SHALE

Extreme Fiction
for Extreme Conditions

SHALE
Extreme Fiction for Extreme Conditions

Edited by
Susan Smith Nash
Nathan Leslie
Valerie Fox
Arlene Ang

*t*P
2015

Texture Press
1108 Westbrooke Terrace
Norman, OK 73072
For ordering information,
visit the Texture Press website at
www.texturepress.org

ISBN-13: 978-0-692-52042-0
ISBN-10: 0-692-52042-2

Printed in the United States of America

Table of Contents

WHAT IS SHALE?

SHALE IS A FINE-GRAINED SEDIMENTARY ROCK THAT FORMS FROM THE COMPACTION OF SILT AND CLAY-SIZE MINERAL PARTICLES THAT WE COMMONLY CALL "MUD". THIS COMPOSITION PLACES SHALE IN A CATEGORY OF SEDIMENTARY ROCKS KNOWN AS "MUDSTONES". SHALE IS DISTINGUISHED FROM OTHER MUDSTONES BECAUSE IT IS FISSILE AND LAMINATED. "LAMINATED" MEANS THAT THE ROCK IS MADE UP OF MANY THIN LAYERS. "FISSILE" MEANS THAT THE ROCK READILY SPLITS INTO THIN PIECES ALONG THE LAMINATIONS.

[GEOLOGY.COM]

The Intruders

• JOEL ALLEGRETTI •

A cigarette and an ashtray appeared on my coffee table alongside the wine carafe from Paris, the twig of coral from a beach in Puerto Rico, and the New Revised Standard Version of the Holy Bible.

The cigarette was unfiltered; it made no pretense about itself. It was half-smoked. The burnt end projected a gray-white curl of ash the length of a baby's pinky. Filaments of tobacco were in a diaspora around the ashtray. If lint were brown, I think it would be tobacco.

The ashtray was a lime-green dollar-store plastic dish. It didn't have the decency to be ceramic or a decorative Japanese plate gone utilitarian. It belonged back in the store aisle with the rest of its kind, not on a glass table sharing square feet with bibelots from France and Puerto Rico in a room with crammed bookshelves and my grandfather's mandolin.

• • •

A week has gone by. The cigarette and the ashtray haven't moved. The carafe, coral, and Bible resent their presence, but like 1980s squatters in an East Village tenement, the duo holds its ground. Because the one who smoked half the cigarette is certain to come back for the other half.

I'm waiting, for no other reason than to see who it was.

Oil Money

• PETER BAROTH •

From the bed all he could see was her back which was carved and muscled in a fine feminine way. On the radio "Love to Love You Baby" droned on in a lazy, narcotic fashion as she lifted her hands over her head in an attempt to manipulate a new hairdo.

"Do you like it up or down?" she asked.

No answer.

She hesitated to the count of two, tilted her head, and then let her bleached hair fall back onto her shoulders. She then reached for a comb from the vanity. She was wearing retro go-go boots along with summer-white shorts, which he figured rarely saw the light of day, and which furrowed in a fashion that rendered them a part of her own sleek lines. He was not really familiar with the garment industry, but he had remembered seeing in his late mother's sewing machine manual that this phenomenon was known as "grinning."

If only he could break a smile himself.

He was Reese Gutman, Radnor, PA. Reared in Houston and Denver and for one year in Duncan, Oklahoma. Daddy in the oil bid'ness. Once for the Shah of Iran, but now for himself. Dad: Meyer, a Hungarian Jewish immigrant to the U.S. with quirky, canny survivor's blood. A soldier in Korea where he had won a bronze star. A one-time school chum of billionaire George Soros, and very nearly as rich. But like Soros, father Gutman was tough-as-nails in his business dealings and elusive, secretive, and withdrawn from a world that still seemed to loom everywhere as a threat to his presence. Reese understood this – that you never again quite trusted a world that had let you down once. With the world as with women. For women were best well-kept and that's what Reese had done with the woman now sitting at the vanity. Room 826, the Charter Hotel, just off 52nd Street, Manhattan. A thousand dollars for a few twilit seconds of raw pleasure. Her name: Stormy Summers. Lissome arms and legs were the means of her game. Stormy Summers, once of Lexington, Kentucky. Stormy Summers of the blonde razor cut, and manicured hands. Stormy Summers, posh prostitute. What was her "legal" name? Well, there was not much legal about her at all.

Yes, Reese had had survivor's blood on that eternally tough, scrapping Jewish side. But tough with a touch of *gimnazium* class and English Premier League soccer tastes.

But Reese's mother had been Christian. And, through her, though never ritually confirmed, Reese had come to realize that he had really been a Christian, too. Gentle, submissive, always prepared to step up to the cross to prove that the world had gone astray. Step up, rather than curl his somewhat delicate fist into a ball and fight, fight, fight the bastards to the end!

Reese had learned to box once, years ago in the quirky streets of West Philly with his running pal and sometime mentor Tyrone Easton. In Ty's rowhouse basement a heavy bag had hung and Reese and Ty had often punched it to their exhaustion - or until their skin, Reese's tan, and Ty's russet, had become sweat-drenched in the draft. Ty had inspired the oilman's son—rendered relaxed and laid-back as a J.J. Cale song by life in the suburban West—to take a shot at survival in the city. Philly had unfurled things for Reese, taught him the frankness of life. If the brutality of Capitalism was veiled, the brutality of the streets was its raw, unfettered cousin. Reese ended up becoming fascinated with street violence; much more so than with the mania of competition at the law school that he was perfunctorily attending.

But Reese was never cut out to be a lawyer. With his parents' approval, Reese had spent so much of his growing years at the sketchpad or practicing the cello—pursuing some notion of scholarship and artistry that seemed apt at the time.

Instead of passing the bar, he pursued writing. He wrote a lot about his experiences out West. Sometimes the subject would be statuesque farmers' daughters and other times it would be the sensation of speed that one might encounter on the endless flats between the Black Mesa and the Sangre de Cristos. He read a little in the burgeoning coffeehouses of the '90s, met creative people, and started to encounter and explore his alienation from what passed for the everyday.

About five weeks before Manhattan, Reese's mood began to

build. There came to be a certain brilliance to his thinking and he started working on two essays: One was on the loss of complexity in the American personality and the other was on the lynch mob as a dominant metaphor in American human relations. Then came the Mystery Tour. A series of events, subjectively real, that Reese's doctor had labeled an "altered state"—a kind of a waking dream. Magical trips into a visionary place—a future containing existential leaps reminiscent of Kierkegaard. Be it craziness or personal evolution, Reese attempted to transform it into writing.

I can imagine what he might have said. He might have conceded that he was affected. But he might also have asked: "What really was *crazy?*" Perhaps there come times, like the '80s, when reality becomes confined into too tight of a place. In terms of physics, when Newton comes to dominate Einstein. When his father's frenzied Capitalist mindset started to choke off his taste for Bartok. But precisely then, what of the ecstasies of a black or Pentecostal Church? What of the fantastic writings of Garcia-Marquez or Borges? What of the animists of Africa?

In a matter of days Reese faced a bout with insomnia. Being unable to sleep, he fell into a kind of daze. A sort of malevolent alter ego appeared. Reese blacks out on a couple of days but remembers exiting the household at 5 a.m. entering his car, destination unknown, cornering, and crashing into a parked car.

Reese Gutman's attorney advised him that the charge of driving under the influence which he faced included being under the influence of prescribed drugs. Shortly before Reese's preliminary hearing the blood test came back positive because of a trace residue of a sleeping pill that Reese had taken hours before. Reese realized what this meant: perhaps as long as a year without a driver's license. To Reese this *also* meant crazy, for in the suburbs this would mean a complete isolation that would truly put him over the edge. He had always fought detachment and this would be its utter form.

The morning of his hearing Reese put on his suit and got into the car. But he didn't turn towards the courthouse. Instead he took a different tack, towards his bank and a withdrawal of $2,000.00. Then he headed up the turnpike to New York City.

As Reese lay on his stomach, the statuesque Stormy Summers approached him from behind. Her orange nails stroked a hypodermic needle.

"Hey, it's one of 'Reese's pieces' here, hon—and I've got *Horse* in my hands," she tittered.

Reese paused and then lunged for a slip of paper lying on the night stand. *Tibor Friedman* it said. *555-596-3810*. A distant cousin, an impoverished filmmaker who worked in a medical equipment store on the Lower East Side to make money. Reese looked at the paper. To call him might mean a chance.

At what?

Reese crumpled up the scrap and threw it on the floor.

El Jardín de los Vampiros

• MARILU BEAS •

En tiempos en que la ciudad de Guadalajara empezaba a crecer y muy poca gente habitaba los suburbios de la ciudad, se desarrollaban nuevas construcciones resaltando entre las pocas casas, compañías con edificios de varios pisos que con sus variadas formas hacían sentir los efectos de modernización.

Recorriendo uno de esos barrios me encontré en medio de dos edificios uno de ellos era un lugar muy especial, parecía un parque y a la vez una de esas residencias antiguas con extensos jardines y árboles enormes que cubren gran parte de la casa y barandales altos que al pasar cerca sientes que la piel se te enchina y te atemorizas pues parece más un cementerio que una casa.

Al acercarme al barandal, me asome y grande fue mi sorpresa pues había muchos niños jugando ahí adentro y se me vino a la mente que quizás fuera un orfanato o una escuela. Sin aguantar más la curiosidad abrí la puerta y entre, era verdaderamente fantástico ver como los árboles mantenían una sombra enorme y sus ramas no dejaban que la luz del sol penetrara, aun así se podía vislumbrar perfectamente a cada uno de los niños y sus pálidas facciones pues no estaban acostumbradas a la luz del día.

Al seguir caminando los rostros de los niños se dirigieron a mí y sin poderlo creer los tenía alrededor mío. Empezó a hablar y ellos nada más se me quedaban viendo.

De repente por la puerta principal aparece un señor muy viejito que apenas podía dar paso, detrás del surge una persona de figura rellenita y bajita, pero con una mirada muy amable. Me preguntaron que se me ofrecía; les conteste que solo iba pasando y me había llamado mucho la atención la casa y sobre todo como estaba habitada de niños, también les pregunte si era un orfanato o una casa hogar para niños desamparados, a lo cual ellos me respondieron que sí que ellos recogían niños

16

House of the Balustrades
• MARILU BEAS •

Translated by Susan Smith Nash*

Back in the times when the city of Guadalajara was just beginning to grow and very few people lived in the suburbs, new buildings started to pop up between the few old houses that remained. Companies with buildings with their varied shapes, sizes, and stories started to feel the effects of modernization.

Roaming around one of those neighborhoods, I found myself between two buildings. One was a very eery place: a park with one of those old residences with extensive gardens and enormous trees that cover a large part of the house and tall balustrades. When you pass close by, you feel your flesh creep and you shudder with mild dread. It looked more like a cemetery than a house.

As I came close to the balustrade, I startled and was very surprised to see children playing inside. It occurred to me that perhaps this place was an orphanage or a school. I was very curious and couldn't resist the temptation to open the door. As I entered, I saw how truly fantastic it was, how the trees cast an enormous shadow, their branches not allowing any sunlight to penetrate. Even though it was dark, I could make out each of the children and their pale features that were not accustomed to the light of day.

As I continued walking, the faces of the children turned to me and I could not believe they were all around me.

Someone started to speak and the children stopped looking at me thanks to the fact that a very old gentleman who could barely walk appeared at the main entrance, and behind him a sweet-faced dumpy little woman. They both asked if they could be of help, and I answered that I was just passing by and the house caught my eye, especially seeing that children lived there. So I also asked if it was an orphanage or a house for disadvantaged children. They immediately said yes and explained that they gathered up

que se la pasaban solamente en la calle mendingando o que no tenían hogar.

En esos momentos hablo la señora bajita y dijo que tenía que marcharse pues la necesitaban en su casa y lo único que lamentaba era quien iba a tender a los niños y al viejito. Sin pensarlo me ofrecí a cuidar de ellos pero tenían que explicarme que es lo que tenía que hacer.

El viejito hablo y dijo que teníamos que presentarnos a lo cual me disculpe pues ni siquiera mi nombre había dado. Les dije que me llamaba Malú y que vivía sola y no tenía a nadie, el viejito se llamaba Arturo y tenía muchos anos atendiendo la casa y a todos los que la habitaban, la señora regordeta llamada Consuelo se encargaba de limpiar y mantener un poco el orden entre ellos, hechas las presentaciones formaron a los chicos y uno por uno fue dando su nombre eran tantos que no pude captarlos, pero pensé que con el paso del tiempo me iría aprendiendo los nombres así como sus gustos y características de cada uno.

Recorrimos la casa y diré que era muy austera y fría, carecía de muebles y olía a humedad, las habitaciones para los niños se encontraban en el piso de arriba las ventanas por fuera parecían como si fueran cuevas y nada mas ellos podían entrar en esa sesión pues según los cuidadores ellos tenían que arreglar sus cuartos así como ocuparse de la limpieza de toda esa sesión y que me daría gusto en no tener que hacerlo yo, pues Arturo era quien revisaba y daba el visto bueno, otra de las cosas que me dijo que no tenía que preocuparme era el de las comidas solamente la mía y del puesto que ellos se preparaban y se alimentaban solos, pues cada quien comía a diferentes horas del día.

Me extraño un poco todo eso y llegue a pensar que esa era la razón por la cual los niños estaban muy pálidos, enseguida pasamos a la cocina, pude observar que era el único lugar de la casa que estaba más iluminada, me explico el viejito que era donde él y Consuelo solían pasar las horas, cosiendo y platicando pues en las mañanas los niños no solían estar alrededor, pregunte la causa y me dijeron que un maestro venia y les daba clases arriba y que algunos de los niños más grandes ayudaban también en instruir.

Concluí que iba a estar muy a gusto pues no me iban a exigir demasiado, además de hacer algo bueno. Pasamos a conocer mi cuarto donde iba a dormir, estaba en la parte de abajo junto con las de Consuelo y Arturo, me dio gusto ver que estaba en buenas condiciones además de tener mi propio baño, me imagine que la

children they found begging in the streets and who needed a home.

The dumpy little woman spoke up and said they had to go now. She needed the children in their house and she was the only one around to take care of them and the elderly man. Without thinking, I offered to take care of them, but they had to explain to me what to do.

The elderly little man asked us to introduce ourselves and I apologized. It had not even occurred to me that I had not even given my name. I'm Malú, I told him, and I live alone, and I have no living relatives. I learned the little elderly man was Arturo and he had been taking care of the house and the occupants for many years. The dumpy little woman was Consuelo and she was in charge of cleaning and keeping everything organized.

Then the children moved into formation and one by one they started giving their names. There were so many I could not catch all of them, but I thought that as time passed I would get to know their names as well as each one of their characteristics and qualities.

We went through the house and I would say it was quite cold and austere. There was not much furniture and it smelled musty. The children's bedrooms were on the floor above the windows. And outside looking in, they looked like little caves. The children were the only ones who could go in that part of the house because, according to the caretakers, they had to pick up their rooms and be responsible for cleaning the entire section of the house. It was a pleasure to me to not to have to do so, since Arturo was the one who would pass through it and give it a good looking-over. Another thing, they said, I did not have to worry about the children's meals. All I had to worry about were my own meals. The children liked to fix their meals by themselves, and besides, each one ate at different times during the day.

Everything seemed strange, and I started think that maybe that was why the children were so pale. We then went into the kitchen, and I could see that it was the only place in the house with lights on. The elderly man explained it was where he and Consuelo tended to kill time, sewing and chatting during the morning when the children weren't around. When I asked why they weren't there, they told me that a tutor came to give classes upstairs, and some of the older children also helped out with teaching.

I concluded that it would be just what I liked and that it wouldn't take too much effort, and plus, I would be doing something good. They then showed me the room where I would be sleeping. It was in the lower

parte de arriba también debería de tener muchas comodidades. Una vez terminado el recorrido, le dije que iba a regresar más tarde pues tenía que ir por mis cosas. Al marcharme me di cuenta que los niños no estaban jugando sino cerca de uno de los árboles y casi no se podían ver, me despedí de Arturo y salí del lugar.

Al regresar de recoger mis cosas había oscurecido, todo estaba muy quieto y no se veía ningún niño fuera de la casa solamente una pequeña luz que se infiltraba por una de las ventanas de abajo y supe que provenía de la cocina, me dirigí hacia allá y solamente me encontré a Arturo comiendo, le pregunte donde estaban los demás y me dijo que se habían ido a descansar y Consuelo ya se había ido a su pueblo.

Me senté a platicar un rato y antes de retirarme a dormir Arturo se me quedo mirando y me dijo muy serio: "Si algún ruido te despierta en la madrugada por ningún motivo salgas de tu habitación, nunca entendiste?"

"Bueno eso es todo por el momento que duermas bien."

Salió sin hacer ruido.

Me fui a mi habitación y me quede pensando en sus palabras, seguí meditando mientras acomodaba mi ropa. Me acosté y enseguida me dormí pues estaba demasiado cansada hasta para pensar. Tendría unas pocas horas durmiendo hasta que empezó a oír ruidos y después aullidos que me erizaban los pelos. Pensé que estaba sonando, pero los oía cerca de mis oídos que no fui capaz ni de abrir los ojos. Los ruidos no cesaron hasta casi amaneciendo. Me desperté mas cansada que cuando me acosté.

Empezó la rutina de hacer de desayunar para Arturo y para mí, había mucha ropa que remendar así que las horas pasaban mas rápidas, hasta que cerca de las cuatro que se suponía que llegaban los muchachos, Arturo siempre me mandaba a comprar algo, así que nunca los vi regresar de sus clases, fui conociendo a los niños por sus nombres y por la forma de comportarse entre ellos había un pequeño que siempre andaba detrás de mí y yo ya me había acostumbrado a la sombra de los árboles.

Un día llegaron unos muchachos más grandes en una camioneta, provocando a los niños, aventando de cosas y sobre todo llamándoles nombres, los niños corrían a ocultarse entre uno de los arboles más grandes, otros subían a las ramas y algunos más corrían a esconderse dentro de la casa. Salí corriendo a tratar de defenderlos y

part of the house, next to Consuelo and Arturo's rooms. I was glad to see it was in good condition and also that I had my own bath. I imagined that the upstairs part of the house must have been very comfortable as well. Once I had finished my trek, I said I'd come back a little later to get my things. As I was leaving, I realized that the children were no longer playing but were doing something around one of other trees. It was hard to make out what was happening. I said goodbye to Arturo and left.

By the time I came back and grabbed my things, it had gotten dark and very quiet. I could not see a single child outside the house. There was just a tiny light that emanated from one of the downstairs windows which I knew came from the kitchen. I headed that way but when I got there, it was just Arturo eating. I asked him where the others were, and he said the children were resting. Consuelo had gone back to her village.

I sat down to chat. Before he headed to bed, Arturo stood watching me, and said very seriously, "If some sort of noise wakes you up at dawn, do not leave your bedroom under any circumstances. Ever. Understood? That's all for now. Sleep well."

He left without making any noise.

I went to my bedroom and I sat thinking about his words. As I arranged my clothes, I continued meditating. I went to bed and being too tired to even think, I immediately fell asleep. I had spent just a few hours sleeping when I started to hear noises, and then howling that made my hair stand on end. I thought that I was dreaming, but I could hear whispering next to my ears. I lay there, unable to open my eyes. The sounds did not cease until almost dawn. I woke up even more tired than when I first went to bed.

That morning, with the routine of making breakfast for Arturo and for myself, then mending items of clothing, the hours flew by. Before I knew it, it was already almost 4 p.m., the time when the children should have been coming back from their classes. Strangely, I never actually saw them come down from their studies. Arturo always sent me off to buy something, just when they should have been returning.

As time passed, I was getting to know the children by their names and their individual quirks and behaviors. Among them, there was a little one who always followed close behind. I was getting used to seeing them in the shadows of the trees.

One day, some older children arrived in a truck, taunting and

gritando que iba a llamar a la policía si no se iban, los ahuyente. Cuando se fueron, de entre las sombras salieron varios niños de los más grandes y musitando dijeron que eso no se iba a quedar así, me les quede viendo a los ojos y su mirada me hizo que me entrara un escalofrió enorme. Como las noches anteriores escuche muchos ruidos, pero esta vez eran muy diferentes eran murmullos y lamentos. Me dispuse a asomarme por la ventana cuando de repente oí ruidos debajo de mi puerta, espere a que tocaran pero nada sucedió, me quede asombrada pues todo estaba en silencio y eso me sorprendió mucho pues desde que había llegado siempre escuche sonidos. Me fui a acostar y me dispuse a dormir trate de concentrarme pero era tanto el silencio que hasta yo misma podía oír el latir de mi corazón.

Pasaron unas horas y apenas estaba empezando a conciliar el sueño cuando escuche demasiado alboroto, me puse mi bata para salir y corrí hasta la puerta de la entrada, abrí la puerta y me quede muda de asombro pues eran todos los niños que estaban reunidos y traían con ellos a los muchachos que los habían atacado. No se dieron cuenta que estaba yo en el marco de la puerta puesto que estaban concentrados. De repente uno de los niños ataco a uno de ellos por el cuello y enseguida los demás se dispusieron a hacer lo mismo con los demás parecían bestias hambrientas y no pequeños seres indefensos. No podía creer lo que veía y en ese momento supe que no eran niños sino vampiros. Tanto fue mi asombro y horror que no sentí que alguien estaba al lado mío, era Arturo, me cubrió la boca para no hacer ningún ruido y me hizo pasar dentro de la casa, fuimos directo a la cocina, me preparo un té y me hizo prometerle que no diría nada de lo que había visto esa noche ni de quien eran los niños, pues sería más peor para mí. Me acompaño a mi habitación y me dijo que no abriera la puerta a nadie, hasta que el no hablara con los niños. No pude dormir de miedo y no me quise levantar temprano. Todo cambio en ese momento para mí, supe que no iba a poder estar ahí y no sentir miedo.

Me levante y me dirigí a la cocina para hablar con Arturo y despedirme, no se encontraba en ella, me dispuse a esperar por él, pues me daba horror tener que caminar por la casa sabiendo que me podían atacar a mi también. Pasaron dos horas y Arturo no aparecía, me empezó a preocupar por él y por no saber si los niños le habían hecho algo. Al poco rato apareció el y traía muy mal aspecto, le hice sentarse e inmediatamente le pregunte que le pasaba, me contesto que ya era su tiempo para retirarse de ese lugar pero antes tenía que dejar a un sucesor y sin

harassing the children, throwing things and calling them names. The children ran to hide in one of the larger trees, and others climbed up the limbs. A few others ran to hide themselves inside the house.

I dashed out of the house, running to try to defend the children, shouting that I would call the police if intruders did not go away. I managed to shoo them away. When they left, out of the shadows emerged several of the larger children who, muttering under their breath, said something about things going on this way. I took a moment to take a look at their eyes and their expressions made me shudder.

That night, like the nights before, I heard noises, but this time they were different, with weird mutterings and moaning. I got ready to look out the window when suddenly I heard noises under my door, and I waited to see if anyone would knock, but nothing happened. Then, to my surprise, the noise ceased, which struck me as strange because I had heard creepy noises at night since the day I arrived. The silence was disturbing. I tried to go to sleep, but it was hard. I tried to focus on sleeping, but the silence was so intense that I could hear my own heart beating.

A few hours passed and I was finally just about to fall asleep when I heard a horrible racket. I grabbed my robe and ran as far as the entryway door. I opened the door and I was left absolutely speechless. All the children had gotten together and they had hunted down, captured, and hauled in the boys who had attacked them. They had no idea I was there. They were all focused on something in the doorframe. Suddenly one of boys savaged one of the children they had brought in, tearing into his neck. Instantly the rest prepared to do the same thing with the others. They looked like hungry wild animals, and not defenseless little beings. I could not believe what I was seeing. Then I knew that they were not children, but vampires.

My shock and horror were so intense that I did not realize that there was someone at my side. It was Arturo, who covered my mouth so I would not make a sound. He guided me inside the house and directly to the kitchen where he made me a cup of tea. He made me promise that I would never tell anyone what I had seen that night, nor who the children were. If I did, it would be all the worse for me.

He went with me to my bedroom and instructed me to not open the door to anyone. He would not say anything to the children. I was too afraid to sleep, and refused to get up early. Everything was completely different

Consuelo para ayudarlo iba a ser mas difícil, además de que ya había hablado con los niños y lo que había sucedido, que no tuviera pendiente pues ellos no me iban a hacer nada. Decidí quedarme hasta que Consuelo regresara, pero le dije que era solamente temporal y no contara conmigo para otras cosas. Armándome de valor salí hacia el jardín y Arturo detrás de mí, no había nadie alrededor pues eran apenas la una de la tarde, me explico que ellos estaban aún durmiendo y que no iban a salir hasta las cinco o seis de la tarde. Tenía muchas preguntas sin respuesta.

Arturo, le dije, vamos a dentro pues necesito que me aclare muchas cosas.

Entramos y nos sentamos uno enfrente del otro y empezó a relatar su historia: Contaba yo veinticinco años cuando me dirigí a la ciudad, venia de un pueblo pequeño en donde todo mundo se conoce y llegar a la ciudad fue un cambio muy grande. Recorrí casa por casa tratando de encontrar un puesto de jardinero o de alguna labor que fuera yo capaz de desarrollar, hasta que entre en esta casa, para eso habían pasado seis meses batallando y haciendo de todo para comer y vivir.

Al llegar a este lugar toque, toque y toque y nadie me respondía hasta que por fin salió una señora ya grande y de aspecto muy cordial que me pregunto que se me ofrecía, de la misma manera que tú entraste en esta casa. Al oírlo me entro un miedo tremendo. Continuando son su relato me dijo que él se enamoró del lugar y que no le importaba no haber tenido una familia propia pues los niños los quería como suyos. También me dijo que fue muy duro el saber que no eran como cualquier niño, en ese entonces había solamente una docena de ellos. El fue recogiendo más niños que andaban por las calles en busca de comida y abrigo y una vez convertidos en vampiros siempre habían sido felices en la manera como Vivian.

Ellos saben que no pueden hacerme nada pues necesitan a una persona que se ocupe de mantener este lugar en buenas condiciones, pues es su casa y su vida que depende de ella. Cuando la viejecita murió me dio este legado que llevo yo desde ese día y que nada ni nadie ha podido quitármelo, ni siquiera ofreciéndome mucho dinero, es por eso que esta casa sigue en pie y seguirá por siempre. Terminada su historia se retiró y quede sola en la cocina.

Medite por mucho rato decidiendo que hacer para no quedarme en ese lugar nada más lo necesario.

No pude hacer nada ese día, cuando llego la hora en que los niños estaban en el jardín, me dije a mi misma que no iba a demostrarles el miedo que sentía

now, and I knew I'd never be able to stay here without feeling raw fear.

I got up and headed to the kitchen to tell Arturo goodbye, but he wasn't there. I waited for him there because it horrified me to walk around the house knowing that the children could attack me as well. Two hours passed and still Arturo had not appeared. I started to worry and wondered if the children had done something. Shortly, he appeared, but he looked ill.

I made him sit down and I asked him what had happened. It was time to get out of that place, he said, but before he left he needed to find a successor. After all, without Consuelo to help him, it was going to be all the more difficult, especially since he had to talk to the children about what had happened. But, there was nothing else pending. They were not going to do anything to me.

I decided to stay until Consuelo got back, but no longer than that. I told Arturo I'd be here for a bit more, but not to count on me for anything else. Bracing myself, I left for the garden with Arturo right behind me. There was no one around, even though it was barely one in the afternoon. I imagined they were still sleeping and that they would not come out until five or six in the evening. I had many questions, but no answers.

"Arturo," I said, "let's go inside. I need you to clear up a lot of things for me."

We entered and sat down one in front of the other and he started to tell me his story.

"Malú, I was 25 when I headed to the city. I came from a small village where everyone knew each other and to be in the city was a big change. I went from house to house trying to find a position as a gardener or any kinds of work I could do, until I came across this house, where I thought I might be able to get some work. By that time, I had spent six months fighting and doing anything to eat and to live.

"Upon arriving at this place, I knocked, knocked, and knocked but no one answered until at last an old woman with a very kind face asked what I was offering. What happened to me was the same as what happened to you. And, I heard the same sound. When I heard it, I was terrified. But, she went on telling me her story. She said that she fell in love with the place and it didn't matter that she didn't have her own family since she loved the children as if they were her own.

"She also told me that it was hard knowing that they were not like

por dentro, así que me fui al jardín y hacer como si nada había pasado. Pero no contaba con que ellos podían oler mi miedo y no dejaban de estar cerca de mi como rodeándome para poder atacar. Hable con algunos de ellos y el niño que siempre me seguía se encontraba más cerca de mí, le susurre que no tenía por qué portarse así, pues yo no le iba a hacer ningún daño ni a él ni a ninguno. Por días se comportaron de esa manera, hasta que un día que Arturo estaba en el jardín y ya había anochecido empezaron a salir de entre las ventanas, parecían que flotaban en el aire y las ventanas me parecieron más tétricas que de costumbre, jamás había visto una cosa así, me quede observando que era lo que hacían.

Empezaron a rodear a Arturo, no podía oír lo que le decían, salí al jardín a averiguar que estaba pasando, Arturo les hablaba con mucho cariño y se estaba despidiendo de ellos, les daba muchas recomendaciones. Cuando por fin termino, volteo, me miro y me dijo:

"A llegado la hora de irme estoy muy viejo y cansado, no voy a aguantar hasta que llegue Consuelo, necesito que estés aquí y cuides de ellos, sé que no debo irme así, pero hoy es el mejor día para despedirme, pues después de esta noche no podría hacerlo. No temas ellos jamás te harían daño. Por favor entra en la casa y no te preocupes, que Consuelo ya sabe lo que tiene que hacer."

Al darme la vuelta para ir a la casa, oí que Arturo les decía:

"Ahora si mis niños, soy suyo, ya saben lo que tienen que hacer."

Espantada me voltee y vi cuando un niño tras otro mordía incansablemente al pobre de Arturo y de él no salía ningún sonido, ni siquiera un lamento. El espectáculo era horrible pues se veía sangre en todos los lugares, sobre todo en el rostro de los niños. Estaba petrificada no podía ni moverme, ni cuenta me di que el niño que me seguía estaba a un lado mío y me tenía agarrada de la mano, no sabía ni que hacer pues era tanto el miedo que tenía que parecía que estaba hipnotizada. En ese momento el niño empezó a morder mi mano y empezó a gritar, le decía que me dejara pero el pequeño no me escuchaba, entre más esfuerzos hacia por librarme de él, más se me pegaba. En esos momentos oímos el rechinar de las puertas del barandal y una voz que gritaba: "no vayan a hacerle ningún daño a Malú", era Consuelo. Jamás en mi vida me dio tanto gusto ver a una persona, todos voltearon hacia ella y se separaron del cuerpo destrozado de Arturo. Consuelo empezó a hablar y les dijo: "Supe cuando me fui que algo de esto iba ocurrir por eso trate de

any other children; and, well, back then there were only about a dozen of them. At any rate, they went on gathering up more children and they traveled the streets in search of food and shelter. Once the children had turned into vampires, everyone was okay with it.

"The children—the little vampires—know that they can't do anything to me and they need a person who will dedicate themselves to keeping this place in good condition. After all, it's their house and their life depends on it. When the old woman died, she left it to me as an inheritance and I have had since then. To this day, nothing and no one has been able to take it from me, not even by offering me a lot of money. So, that's why this house keeps going and it will keep going forever."

Once Arturo finished the story, he headed to bed and I was left alone in the kitchen.

I mulled over what I could possibly do so I would not have to stay in this place any longer than necessary.

I could not do anything that day, and when the hour came when the children were in the garden, I told myself I was not going to show them any of the fear I really felt. I headed to the garden and acted as though nothing had happened. But I did not take into consideration the fact that they could smell my fear. They kept coming toward me, and I could tell they were positioning themselves to surround me so they could attack.

I spoke with a few of them, and the boy that always followed me was closest. I whispered to him that he did not have to act that way, after all I was not going to harm him or the others in any way. For days, they behaved in that way, to the point that one day when Arturo was in the garden and when night was falling they came out from between the windows. They seemed to float in the air, and the windows seemed darker and more morose than they usually were. I had never seen anything like it, and I stood there, trying to make out what they were doing.

They started to surround Arturo and I could not hear what they said. I left the back yard to see what was going on. Arturo was saying something, and he was doing it really sweetly and with intense tenderness. I could tell he was saying goodbye. And, he was giving them a few final words of guidance and advice. When he finally finished, he turned, saw me, and said, "The time has come for me to go away. I'm very old and tired, and I'm not going to make it until Consuelo gets back. I need for you to be here and to take care

venirme lo más pronto que pude pero aquí estoy yo y los voy a cuidar y proteger como Arturo lo hacía, no voy a permitir que algo les pase, pero dejen ir a Malú".

El niño que me tenía agarrada de la mano, le contesto: "Eso no es posible pues desde que llego a este lugar, siempre quisimos que se hiciera como nosotros y la empezamos a querer, así que aunque ella quiera irse no podrá pues al chuparle yo de la mano, automáticamente ya es una de las nuestras y vivirá con nosotros por todo el tiempo, además que podrá estar entre los dos mundos, el del día y el de las tinieblas."

Al oír eso no pude contenerme más y salí corriendo de esa casa sin rumbo fijo y jure nunca volver.

* Translator's Note: After putting together a "literal" translation, I decided to try a more "fluid" translation that would capture the art and suspense of the story. In doing so, I was embracing Lawrence Venuti's ideas about translation, and following the literary examples of Ezra Pound and Louis Zukofsky. The author reviewed the translation and was happy with it—I hope the readers enjoy it as well.

of them. I know I shouldn't take off like this, but today's the best day to say goodbye since after this night, I won't be able to do so. Don't be afraid of them. If you're not afraid, they'll never hurt you. Please go in the house and don't worry. Consuelo already knows what has to happen."

When I turned to go toward the house, I heard Arturo say, "Now my children, I'm yours. You know what you have to do."

Shocked, I turned and I saw one child after another mercilessly and tirelessly feed on poor Arturo. Not one sound issued from him, not even one shriek of pain or terror. The scene was ghastly with blood everywhere, but more than anything, all over their faces.

I was petrified and could not even move and I did not even realize it when the child that always followed me was at my side and had grabbed me by the hand. I did not know what to do, and I was so terrified I felt hypnotized. The child began to bite my hand. I screamed and told him to leave me alone, but the little one did not listen to me. The more I tried to get free, the tighter he held on.

Then the outside gates opened and a voice shouted: "You are not going to do anything that will cause any harm to Malú!" It was Consuelo.

Never in my life had I been so happy to see a person. All of them turned toward her and pulled themselves away from Arturo's mutilated body.

Consuelo began to speak and she told them: "I knew that when I left that something was going to happen! That's why I tried to come back as quickly as I could. It took some time, but here I am. I'm going to care for you and protect you like Arturo did. I'm not going to let anything happen to you. But you need to let Malú go."

The child gripping my hand answered, "No way! We liked her the minute we met her, and we wanted her to become like us so she would not be able to leave. She wants to leave, but she can't. She does not know it, but I bit and sucked her hand. Now she's one of us and will live with us all the time. Plus, she'll be able to move between the daylight and the twilight worlds. It's perfect."

When I heard that, it was too much.

I couldn't hold myself back for even one second longer, and I took off running from that house. I had no idea where I was going or how, but I swore that I would never, ever, come back.

Intervals in Moonglow
• ANNIE BIEN •

I peel off moments into my diary:

DAY/NIGHT 1. INTERVAL WITH THE SMALL THINGS

I dreamt you led me between two walls, very narrow, my head wouldn't fit even if I sucked my stomach in—then you pulled my hand—

A door opens and shuts. I try to hide, then see it's you—Mommy— no longer dead from five years before. My right hand clasps yours—once mine fit into your palm:

> *Your breath barely grazed the pillow that last day, you only slept. I remembered the times you sang me to sleep. Your hand patted my arm to a distracted tune from your childhood as your eyes gazed upon the waves sweeping your memories into Repulse Bay . . . When walking the hill overlooking the hospital, the moon swelled in magnificent relief, magnifying our temporary state. I didn't want to disturb you in the room; I wanted to be uplifted, just in case it was the last day—just in case it was not. Some tears fell, these are the it's-okay-to-go-don't-feel-burdened-by-us tears. I have heard from the lamas that you hear everything when death is near—voices may babble but all thoughts are sonorous. This is when verbs are infinite and you read all minds . . .*

Then—sweat under the covers—blue illuminated 4:30 AM—a radio announcer dissolves our hand-clasped dream-state. I awaken: Heart-pounding-into-dawn-consciousness is reluctant to leave your visitation. Good-bye.

NIGHT/DAY 2. INTERVAL WITH THE MEDIUM THINGS

We have not yet met in this moment, though once my most-beloved from my future and a non-remembered enemy in my past, or perhaps once most-beloved-reluctantly lost in my past and unwilling-to-accept-as-enemy in the future.

Here you stand in front of me: one eye glistens blue and the other flecked with gold sparks on a green sea. Some gust of wind blows a curl over your brow. Before I fell asleep, I thought fleetingly of the space between imagination and reality: the tip of your head. Turning away from the optical eye to the mind's eye, unjudged by conventional reality as real. You walk toward me, my friend from infinite rebirths.

This jungle vine mixed with camellias, the steam of the greenhouse and dirt on the garden floor, the art deco room in the middle of the Victorian house that opens onto a view of the Woolworth building—you reassure me, this is as real as being awake is fleeting. Sometimes when here, in this recurring dreamworld, I am alone, searching for the center of the mandala. But this time, you drape your coat around me. I am the unseen shadow, you are vivid, tall. From the window, we watch the clouds obscure and reveal cityscape, blown by a cool breeze. My arms hold your waist, your arms, a banyan tree, embrace me. Such is your visitation, the main character who fell out of the sky into my notebook. Before so vague, now I hear your voice, a low amused murmur sharing a secret; the veins on the back of your right hand, your long fingers entwine mine.

DAY/NIGHT 3. INTERVAL WITH A GREAT THING

At the crown of your head, a small Buddha glows, radiant, his eyes hover over your third eye: the place between your brow vibrates. The light of sunrise on morning clouds, pink, iridescent, of no visible light source, pours down through the crown of your head. Golden nectar infuses your body. Radiant sparks catch sunlight from golden skin and the voice of your teacher melts into you, suffusing your mind with dawn sky. The moment vanishes, as you do, into molecules, into atoms, into universe, and stars, acacia trees, sandalwood forests, the buds on the narcissus not ready to bloom, ice caps, the polar bear breathing a cloud of cold, the whale diving away from the debris left over the surface of the earth, the sloth clinging to a vine, upside-down, a snake winding its way as the liana. Your mind settles upon a tiny glowing syllable, *HUM*, growing in brightness. The shape of the letter begins to erase itself from bottom to top—*OOH*, the sounds seems to say—*HAA*—a release of breath, *MMM*—eases into an echo radiating outwards as the universe. The tiny Buddha mixes into flesh, blood, bones, his smile fans the body. You look up. It is the same room you have lived in for years, the cats running across the hardwood floor murmuring and squeaking—because one doesn't know how to meow, the other translates into purr and wow. Yet it is a totally new room, new dust alights in old places. Arising from an abandoned fixed view, the room is veiled by sameness. On this evening, the clouds obscure the sun and ebbing daylight announces the everyday pond of fish swimming among reeds—flicking tales of infinite lives. I hear my fingers tap, my witnesses to fragile remembrance.

New Year's Eve

• PETER BYRNE •

It must have been about 6:30 when Flynn opened his eyes. Thick sunlight poured into the room, unobstructed by shades. Shades would have impeded the cool night-time breezes that offered some respite from the penetrating heat of Colombia's Caribbean coast. In 1981, few homes in Barranquilla had air conditioning.

His buddy Gerardo had suggested he visit Barranquilla on his way back from Christmas holidays in the US. Both were students in Bogota at the country's most exclusive private university. Flynn reasoned that Gerardo's family was rich. An engineering student, Gerardo was fun, but soft-spoken and kind. Flynn eagerly accepted the invitation. Four days to see the land of Garcia Marquez, the place where the mighty Magdalena River empties into the sea. He imagined dinners at a country club. Maybe Gerardo's family would take him sailing.

Things were not proceeding according to plan. Flynn was somewhere between uncomfortable and miserable.

He had flown in late Tuesday night, 30 hours before. Only 3 weeks earlier he had seen Gerardo in Bogota, but now they were on holiday in Gerardo's home town. So they went straight from the airport to a bar. Flynn was up early yesterday, ready to see the sights. But no one else stirred until mid-morning. And last night, Flynn drank too much. To be more precise, last night was the culmination of a drinking session with Gerardo's extended family that started before lunch and continued for twelve hours. An assortment of cousins, aunts, uncles and friends of all ages came and went. Most had heard Flynn was visiting, and this provided a rare opportunity to see a live gringo. The beer, rum and poisonous *aguardiente* flowed. Flynn was on display and had to be sociable.

Flynn was hung over, but the greater problem was lack of sleep. For the holidays, the sleep schedule for Gerardo's family was 2AM-10AM. This would be no problem if Flynn were not cursed with a brain that shifted into gear at 6AM no matter when he had gone to sleep. This was his second night of scant sleep. Two more to go, and tonight was New Year's Eve. *What a relief it will be to get back to Bogota. Fifty-six hours.* But still, this should be fun. If only he could sleep.

Two small lizards rested on the walls of chipped yellow paint. *Lizards are good, they eat insects. Definitely too many bugs here.* There were no screens on the windows. He closed his eyes and scratched his mosquito bites.

It was already getting hot. *Just relax, maybe fall asleep again.* But no, Flynn's restless mind and the sun-filled room conspired against sleep. He opened his eyes again and looked around. He occupied one of four rickety beds spread around a bare room. Three other bodies, slumbering peacefully. There was Gerardo, soft-spoken and kind. *How could he be the son of the man I met yesterday?*

Sr. Rivas was the stereotypical buffoon that people in Bogota identified with people of the Caribbean coast. Impulse ruled Sr. Rivas, or so it appeared. He embraced Flynn as a fourth son (or fifth, or sixth?) from the moment they met. Most Colombians liked Flynn's name—it was so American, yet they could pronounce it easily. Or so they thought—it was uniformly pronounced "Fleen". He even introduced himself as Fleen- it was unique, unlike his first name. But Rivas simply called him "Gringo".

Rivas had been absent yesterday morning. When he arrived around lunch-time, he insisted on booze for all, including his 13 year-old son. It was obvious that the drinking, smoking, etc. had commenced somewhat earlier for Rivas. His presence in the house was like a tornado. Riotous laughter, singing, hugging, smoking, dancing, drinking . . . and then he was gone. There were three more of these visits over the course of the afternoon and evening. Each time he brought different people. On one of these visits he was accompanied by Oscar, whom Gerardo introduced as his brother. Flynn thought he had already met Gerardo's brothers. Oscar evidently shared his father's attitude toward life, and Rivas was more affectionate with Oscar than with his other sons. Of the sons, Oscar alone had an Afro-Caribbean aspect. Neither Gerardo's father nor mother appeared to have any black blood.

They were all so nice. Rivas would occasionally take note of Flynn, wave his cigarette or drink theatrically and shout "GRINGO, THEES

EES YOUR HOUSE!" This stirring declaration represented Rivas's total knowledge of English, and he made frequent use of it. Everyone else spoke Spanish—but not the clear, elegant Spanish of Bogota. In Barranquilla the words surged out in a loud, messy torrent. Familiar words were rendered unrecognizable, and every sentence was peppered with local slang. Flynn felt like a beginner, not someone whose Spanish was good enough for college classes in Bogota. He strained to understand as the guests pelted him with information and questions. At first he was dismayed. Then he realized that these people were talkers, not listeners. They spoke, Flynn smiled and drank. Everyone was happy.

After Oscar and Rivas blew out again, Flynn asked whether Oscar was older or younger. Gerardo had been completely natural with Oscar, but his faced darkened at this question. In a low voice he responded "Oscar is five months older than I am. He lives with his mother."

It seemed to Flynn that Gerardo was not embarrassed by his father's indiscretions. Nor was he bothered that his father seemed to favor Oscar. He was embarrassed that a foreigner like Flynn could never understand what was normal in this world.

Flynn felt sweat accumulating in several places. One of the lizards ran down the wall and out of sight.

As the others slept, the words of a catchy, popular song drifted through his head: "*Mis amigos me tienen rabia, porque tengo dos mujeres/ my friends are pissed off, because I have two women.*" Gerardo explained: the singer's friends were jealous, not self-righteous. Having women on the side was like getting drunk. The women did not like it, yet their tolerance and participation made it possible.

These men led joyous, unconstrained lives. They slept peacefully, for they did not worry about tomorrow. Flynn was baffled and amused, envious and sickened.

There was no indication that Rivas, now in his mid-forties, was slowing down. Gerardo and his younger brothers were so calm by comparison. No mystery: Señora Rivas was a *dama*, a lady. She was sweet, serious, and evidently dedicated to home and family. She probably prayed for her husband's soul every night. And Rivas likely married her because she reminded him of his own departed mother. No doubt he intended to be the husband she deserved . . . at some point in the future. And no doubt she would forgive him in the unlikely event he ever made it to that point.

It was now 7:15. Exasperated, Flynn shut his eyes. He knew he would not sleep.

A car approached the house. Silence, followed by faint, slow footsteps. Silence. Then the door to the bedroom burst open, and Rivas flashed across the room toward the bed of his youngest son. Before the boy could react, Rivas dug his fingers into his ribs and tickled him mercilessly. Rivas laughed hysterically, the boy laughed uncontrollably. The two older sons laughed sleepily but assumed more defensive positions on their beds. Flynn laughed nervously.

New Year's Eve had begun.

O' Baptism, Sings the River
• LISA J. CIHLAR •

Crowhead dives into the plungepool. He has no pockets for stones. The chlamys adds to the weight of fall-water crashing over his shoulders. There is a burden to the baptism. He must bring forth a clam with a half-formed pearl to pass to his torturer. She will wear it away by thumb-rubbing it year after year. She never feels the final grit of sand that started the bead. It slips off the shine of button-shell and leaks out of a careless, wide stitch of the pouch made from pale-cream and soft tanned deer hide. Her father created the bag for her and she feels indebted to him for this and all the gifts he handed down. Everything is genetics, he proclaims on all of her birthdays. If he says it often enough and loud enough she will come to believe him. Crowhead feels the water with him everywhere. He bears it like a minor god.

A Dish Best Served Unnoticed

• JAMES CLAFFEY •

Traipsing about, the city under threat of rain. Those clouds—amazing thunderheads rolling over the Dublin Mountains—the thick accumulation of gray a thumbed smudge print on a child's exercise book. I had pulled it together since you'd left me, my pride swallowed. I'd begun meetings in the Protestant hall—"Getting to Grips with Your Anger"—and had even shared several of the embarrassing tales of your mistreatment. It never struck me that you were the one needing help, consumed as I was by a love in blinders. That time you slapped me on the side of the head with the stapler: blurred vision and three stitches. The other time you twisted my arm behind my back and fucked my shoulder up. The gang all said I'd be better off leaving you, though I thought differently, dogged bastard that I am. There was a moment when I expected you to murder me in my sleep. A zip file of each of the times you beat me, or threatened me, or pretended to, is hidden in my office at work—just in case. Your taste in clothes kept me chained to the dog post of your love. Those patterned dresses, diaphanous and tormenting, acted like a sedative to me, and the pathetic knucklehead in me refused to accept the obvious truths raining down on my bruised torso. In the cool afternoons when you were away surfing I prayed to the Virgin Mary and the Christ Child, solitary prayers of revenge, prayers summoning up sneaker waves of revenge to suck you below and fill your breathless lungs with water.

Mad Dogs & Irishmen

• JAMES CLAFFEY •

The Old Man keeps his teeth in a Rothman's ashtray, surrounded by butts and match ends. It creeps me out, and explains the dental problems that have resulted in the erosion of his entire upper set of gums. The flesh is a caramelized black fatty-like consistency, and his inability to chew properly leads to the malnutrition that has Mam so worried she's taken to feeding him with an ancient baby bottle, replete with rubber nipple.

"They're helpless when they're born and they make their way back to helplessness as the years go by," she says.

Added to his gum problems is the state of his eyes: one clouded by a cataract, and the other stitched shut from where he'd been clubbed in the head on the oil rig back in the 70s. In effect the Old Man is as blind as a headless chicken and he often falls over the dog on his way to the outside toilet. When this happens, the dog, who is named DeValera after the president, rises up and paws at the Old Man's belly with his claws.

The Old Man spends his last years with long scars on his belly from the dog's clawing and declares that he'll "declaw the Fianna Fáil bastard," if it'd stand still long enough. DeValera is as slippery a customer as his human namesake, and skips out of harm's way any time the Old Man gets close. The one time he does manage to grab the mongrel by its collar, the mange-ridden beast buries its teeth in the Old Man's hand, causing frantic scenes in the kitchen, where Mam pours Mercurochrome on the wound and bandages it in a clean tea towel. We hide the dog for a month in the coal shed for fear the Old Man will have him destroyed. When DeValera reappears it's with a jet-black coat instead of the lighter fawn color he's sported since we'd got him from one of the Old Man's customers.

Mam tires of the teeth in the ashtray, particularly when she arrives in from the shops and finds the Old Man asleep in his favorite chair and

DeValera gnawing on the false teeth. It takes a good half hour to finesse the teeth from the dog and not wake the Old Man for fear of him having the dog's guts for garters. When she finally frees the falsies, Mam soaks them in Jeyes' fluid to clean them and I work them with a sheet of fine sandpaper to take out the teeth marks.

The last straw is when DeValera chews through the Old Man's bamboo fly rod, and the once-shiny instrument splinters into bits. The Old Man is a dab hand at the angling, and the fishing equipment he keeps in the pantry under the stairs is his pride and joy. When he finds DeValera slobbering over the rod there is slim to no chance the dog will survive the night.

Wrong or right, the Old Man calls to one of his old buddies and the dog is taken away in the back of a Boland's bread van. A queer sadness permeates the house for months after, and the Old Man sucks on the dog-bitten false teeth and curses both DeValera's: man and dog.

Mothering

• JAMES CLAFFEY •

Revolve, through sinewy trails of hanging plants, through the mildewed roach-filled denim wall friezes she once thought lent an air of serenity to her home. Mam found her taste in the pages of Woman's Weekly, and Ireland's Own, buried in the jiggery-pokery of lurid stories of nurses and doctors in breathless clinches. I grew up crunching on the horsehair stuffing of our dilapidated sofa, the one with long tears on the cushions. I was a small child, a boneheaded brat with an occasional large bump on my forehead where I walked into a door, later calmed and soothed by the butter mother rubbed on the goose-egg. My hollers went unchecked, my fingers caught in various places of torture—the accordion hinges of the old gramophone table, between the rollers of the mangle in the laundry room—my misbehavior often punished by an early trip under the bed covers. Some nights the sun would still be shining in the window, the smell of the Robin's starch from Mam's ironing wafting up the stairs. She ironed *everything*, even Da's underpants. Jockey Y-fronts. Her day was never done. Bake soda bread, fold linen, smoke one cigarette after another, the puffs fast and taut. She strode about the house; butt clenched between her lipsticked teeth, polishing the squares of the tiled bathroom wall, waxing the dining room table, a day's work never done. Outside my window, the neighborhood girls played hopscotch, singsong cries floating upwards, the sinking of the sun giving way to the darkening of sky and coming of moon.

A LADY

• LYDIA CORTES •

THERE'S A LADY/ IN HER 50s/ COULD BE 60s/ SHE'S DRESSED
ACTUALLY MORE SWADDLED IN LAYERS/ SWOLLEN IN OVER-
SIZE BLACK SWEAT PANTS/ LIME GREEN JACKET WITH NEON
WHITE STRIPES/ HOOD COVERS HEAD UNDER SHE WEARS A
BLACK SKULL CAP/ WHITE *PUERTO RICO* LETTERS STAMPED
ACROSS ONE SIDE TO THE OTHER/ I DON'T KNOW SHE'S A
LADY/ WE PRs SAY LADY A LOT/ WOMAN STANDS A BLOCK
BELOW CANAL NEAR POST OFFICE/ SHE HOLDS AN ORANGE
FLAG SHE NOW AND THEN WAVES/ MAYBE SHE'S A SCHOOL
CROSSING GUARD/ BUT IN THAT PART OF SOHO ONCE FACTO-
RY TOWN THERE'S NO SCHOOL YET NOT EVEN A POSH PRIVA-
TE ONE AS BEFITS CURRENT NABE/ WHAT THE HELL/ WHY IS
SHE STANDING THERE IN THE CRUELTY OF THIS MIDWINTER
DAY/ I LOOK UP/ SEE THEY'RE PUTTING UP ANOTHER FANCY
HIGH-RISE BUILDING FOR HIGH-RISEN FANCY PEOPLE/ GONE
THE PEOPLE WHO WORKED IN FACTORIES/ THE MANUFAC-
TURING AND PRINTING BUSINESSES/ GONE SHOPS FULL
OF TRIMMINGS AND BUTTONS ONCE OWNED BY HASIDICS/
THEN IT HITS ME/ SHE'S THERE TO WARN ANY ONCOMING
TRAFFIC OF BUILDING GOING UP/ CAUTION PASSERSBY CARS
ABOUT ANY METAL SCAFFOLDING PIECES/ HAMMERS THAT
MIGHT RAIN DOWN/ OR SOME UNFORTUNATE NON-UNION

IMMIGRANT LABORER PLUNGING UNINTENTIONALLY KILLING MORE THAN JUST HIMSELF/ AGAINST GUSTS I CROSS WOOSTER AND GRAND/ PUSH TOWARD CANAL ST PO/ NEED TO PICK UP WHO KNOWS WHAT/ A LETTER/ PACKAGE/ PAPERS TO SIGN/ MAILPERSON LEFT PINK SLIP IN MY BOX/ SHE WON'T COME AGAIN/ ALREADY KNOW HER/ GOT ATTITUDE/ SO MUST PICK UP OR IT'LL GO BACK/ WHAT IT COULD BE/ SOMETHING I DON'T WANT/A SUMMONS/ A BIBLE/ DON'T NEED JURY DUTY/ MAYBE SOMETHING IMPORTANT/ PASSING THE GUARD I POINT TO HER CAP/ IN ENGLISH SAY *THIS SURE AIN'T PR*/ BLANK LOOK/ I REPEAT IN SPANISH *ESTO SI QUE NO ES PUERTO RICO!*/ STILL STARES LIKE CAN'T MAKE OUT WHAT THE HELL I'M SAYING/ I REMEMBER THAT I DON'T LOOK PR (SO THEY SAY)/ MAYBE THINK I'M NOT SUPPOSED TO SPEAK HER SPANISH/ THAT I'M SOME WHITE WEIRDO IN MY LONG DESIGNER COAT OF MANY COLORS DIFFERENT FABRICS PATCHES SEWN TOGETHER/ TIES AND LOOKS LIKE A BATHROBE/ COULD BE THINKING ONLY UNA AMERICANA LOCA WOULD WEAR THAT/ OR COULD CARE LESS ABOUT DESIGNER COATS/ FROM THE BIT OF SKIN I CAN SEE SHE'S LIGHT SKINNED TOO/ SHE DOES LOOK PUERTORRIQUEÑA TO ME/ WHAT WITH THE PR HAT/ BUT MAYBE I'M WRONG/ COULDN'T SHE BE A BRIGHTON BEACH RUSSIAN/ SOME RECENTLY ARRIVED EASTERN EUROPEAN IMMIGRANT/ DOESN'T THEIR ADVANCED EDUCATION LAND THEM CHOICE UNION JOBS RIGHT AWAY/ FASTER THAN MANY PRs HERE MANY YEARS/ LIKE THIS ONE WHO GETS TO STAND IN THE BITTERNESS AND WAVE DANGER AWAY/ MAYBE SOMEHOW THIS RUSSIAN LADY OR WOMAN CAME ACROSS THE WARM CAP SELLING FOR

REAL CHEAP/ SO CHEAP SO GOOD A DEAL SO WHAT IF IT SAID PUERTO RICO/ WE STARE AT ONE ANOTHER EACH WITH HER OWN PRESUMPTIONS/ THEN SHE FINALLY SPEAKS/ SAYS *QUE* / SO I REPEAT IN ENGLISH THEN IN SPANISH/ SAY HOW DIF-FERENT THIS WEATHER IS FROM PRs/ I POINT TO HER CAP/ SHE THEN PUTS DOWN HER HOOD/ PULLS THE CAP AWAY FROM HER EARS/ REMOVES EAR BUDS/ HOW COULD I KNOW SHE WAS LISTENING TO MUSIC/ SHE SMILES SAYS *OH SI ESTO SI QUE NO ES PUERTO RICO MIJA/ NO VEO LA HORA CONSE-GUIR MI SOCIAL SECURITY/ ENTONCES RAPIDO RAPIDITO ME REGRESO A MI BELLA BELLISIMA ISLITA/* I SMILE ALMOST HUG HER/ OH TO BE UNDERSTOOD/ IN ENGLISH I WISH HER A GOOD DAY/ SAY *CUIDADO KEEP WARM/* SHE SMILES AGAIN PUTS THE FLAG UNDER HER ARM RUBS HER GLOVED HANDS/ SHE SAYS THE SAME BACK TO ME *CUIDATE TAKE CARE/* THEN ADDS *QUE DIOS TE BENDIGA/* ONE CAN'T GET MORE PUERTO RICAN THAN THAT/ I'M MOVED TO TEARS BY HER WORDS/ EVEN IF I DON'T BELIEVE IN GOD IT'S SUCH A KIND CARING BLESSING/ COSA DE FAMILIA.

Tempera in the Kitchen
• DANIELA ELZA •

Jenny often heard the word ego, and she wondered what it looked like. She pictured different things but the most prominent were the images of storms and monsters. Many times she wondered what color it was. Probably it was the same color as angry, for every time it would come up her parents would fight over it.

"You have it," said her mother. "No, you've got it," said her father. Well, she couldn't understand why anyone would keep it.

Jenny finally decided to ask her mom, since dad kept saying she had it most of the time. She needed enough details to picture it. Then she could draw it.

"What color is the ego, Mom?" asked Jenny, standing in the middle of the kitchen floor hugging her favourite teddy bear, Burny. Kate was washing the dishes and kept dipping her hands in the brown residue, a sign that her husband had cooked that night.

"It's, um, a dirty brown color," she said, raising her voice hoping that John would hear. After a few minutes she said in a softer voice, "There are other colors too, Jenny. The ego is not just one color. Depending on its size. When it is small it could be blue, green or pink, it could be yellow or orange, it can even be warm and soft like Burny," Kate nudged the teddy bear with her elbow for her hands were dripping soap and went on, "When it's big it's scary and it can be very destructive. Like our river Jenny, you know, when it overflows and soaks up our backyard. Remember the time when it drowned the tomatoes?"

"Is it like a brown monster?" asked Jenny, pursing her eyebrows together.

"Yes, something like that and you have to give sacrifice to it."

"Why do you fight with Dad over the ego, if it is so terrible?" asked

Jenny.

"Because I have to sacrifice myself," answered Kate, beginning to feel uncomfortable.

"But Dad says you have it," persisted the little girl.

Kate dried her hands and kneeled before Jenny. "Dad is conflicted, he doesn't mean what he says. He loves you very much, you have to be sure of that. He wouldn't let a hair fall off your head. Don't judge him too harshly." Jenny took a deep sigh. "I don't like the way he shouts at you and . . . when he wants to hit you."

Kate reached out and enveloped her daughter in a deep hug saying softly in her ear, "He doesn't mean to hurt me Jenny. He just has a bad temper!"

Jenny wondered over Kate's shoulder what color temper was and how could her dad be so careless as to get bad temper. She asked, "Is Daddy ill from bad temper, Mom?"

"Something like that," answered Kate not being able to figure where this whole conversation was going.

Jenny was not giving up. "But if he is ill why isn't he in the hospital, or suffering from being ill?"

Kate squeezed Jenny tighter and the lump in her throat didn't let out what she took a deep breath to say. Instead she fidgeted with the teddy bear and found to her dismay that the bear's face was gone. It looked as if it was scooped out and instead of a face there was a huge blackness gaping at her.

"What happened to Burny?" she asked puzzled.

"Oh, he was just being a pain. So he lost his face. He deserved it," said the soft angel face staring openly and innocently into Kate's terrified eyes.

They Will Call Her Shaya

• SHINELLE L. ESPAILLAT •

He hated malls. He also hated people. But he had to brave holiday shoppers to buy his wife a gift, even though this year nothing he bought would matter. She would likely not even open it.

So much did he hate malls and people that once he finally found a spot in the dark garage, he parked and sat with his head on the wheel for half an hour, no music, just his heart beating in his ears, until someone knocked on the window.

"You gotta pay for the spot." He lifted his head and saw a yellow-vested rent-a-cop, whose face folded in on itself when she saw his, and she took a step back. He wiped his eyes with his sleeve. He got out, and Yellow-vest took another step back. "Maybe you should go on home. We don't want trouble in here."

He didn't want trouble in here either. He could have told Yellow-vest that he didn't want to be there at all, that his wife was a ball of pain in a dark room, that he only hoped that somehow soothing her hurt would soothe his. Instead, he told her he would be quick. He walked away, paid at the damn parking meter and headed for Sears, knowing that nothing he bought would mean anything.

Hard knots of women scavenged the landscape. He took a few vague steps, only to have sharp elbows nudge him aside. He kept trying, though he moved as though under sedation, and the lights made him feel undead. He slogged through a clotted maze of women's clothing before affirming that he knew nothing about women's clothing, and that anyway a sweater would not be the panacea she needed. He asked two different men how to get to jewelry, but they each just waved him in a direction—east or north, or just away. Of the million sweaty shrieking people swarming through this space, approximately none of them worked there. He felt like a lion in a stampede of gazelles.

He walked. He didn't have a map, he couldn't find a directory, he couldn't hold onto a complete thought, but he kept moving, because he believed that in department stores, ultimately all roads lead to jewelry, and it turned out that he was right. He stumbled into a small city of glass cases and spinning towers. He reached for something glittery—he didn't even know what it was—but someone snatched it from him, and the edges sloughed some skin off his fingerprints. He was failing.

He was shaking, and he leaned against a pillar to keep himself from falling. He started to lower his head into his hands, but then he caught a glimpse in a mirror of something perfect. He hesitated; he didn't want to move toward it only to have someone else snatch it away. But nobody moved in, nobody else saw it or wanted it, and for the first time in a month he was hopeful. He wiped his eyes and began to move, slowly. He was a little afraid of what he could do. This would make his wife get out of bed, smile, *live*.

He picked up the child and pressed his fingers to her lips. Nobody saw, nobody said a word to him. He carried her out of the store, and he was crying yet again, but it was okay. This would mean something. This would matter.

Excerpt from *On the Gold Coast*
• EVALD FLISAR •

Translated by Timothy Pogacar

Before Sylvia decided to study physical therapy, she saw herself as a zookeeper. Or better, one that fed the animals, was friends with them and a part of their lives. She would visit a zoo at least once a month. And when she started traveling in Europe, first by herself and then with Peter, a visit to the zoo was always at the top of the list. She had three photo albums at home for just animals, from tigers to moles, from mice to rhinos, from eagles to snakes. She feared snakes the most, even though they fascinated her. She bought an illustrated encyclopedia of animals in twenty-five volumes on credit; she wanted to know the entire animal kingdom.

She discovered how dry the academic view of animals was only after she came across the chapter about African wildlife in Hladnik's book *A Call Without an Echo*. There the animals came alive. She felt them as if they were all gathered in her yard. It was obvious that Hladnik loved them, perhaps more than people. He wrote about them with a tenderness that overshadowed all other distinctions in his writing. He knew the African fauna especially well, as if he had spent half his life in the wilderness.

Sylvia's only demand at the start of the African trip—one she wouldn't negotiate with Peter—was to visit the Waza National Park. It was sixty kilometers north of Maroua. Pedestrians were not allowed because the lions would certainly have them for lunch, which would significantly reduce the number of new tourists. Besides, the park was not a zoo where you can stroll from cage to cage in half an hour. In the guidebook Peter found that the Waza National Park had over 70,000 hectares and was for the most part covered by open savanna.

A cab driver by the name of Amado offered to drive them there for twelve thousand francs. Sylvia was all for it, but Peter thought it was a rip off. Next day three cab drivers demanded twice as much, and two others even more. They searched for Amado in the dusty streets of the city the entire day but couldn't find him. Then they found out at the travel agency that a group of European tourists was coming by plane from Douala the next day. The Norcamtour agency was driving them to Waza for a two-day excursion; if they wanted to, they could join. They paid seventeen thousand francs apiece.

The tour bus picked them up at five in the morning at Le Relais Porte Mayo, where they had returned after a week at the Jovanovićs', and drove them to the Novotel, where the European safari participants were staying. They could see through the dining hall windows that they were having breakfast. They sat in the bus and waited. The bus was very small, for fifteen persons at most, but it had comfortable seats, which seemed to Peter extremely important, while Sylvia was more interested in how close up they would see the lions.

When the tourists started to get on, they were unpleasantly surprised by the couple's presence. They stared, exchanged glances, and cast around comments in French. Finally a Norcamtour employee rudely ordered them to move to a similar bus parked behind the first. They grabbed their bags and moved. The other bus was still empty. When tourists started getting in, their surprise was even greater. An arrogant black woman haughtily remarked that they were sitting in her place and should go to the first bus. Since she was the only black person among the travelers, they assumed that she, too, was a Norcamtour employee, so they listened. But the first bus was already full.

The driver led them back to the second one. Peter was trying to explain to him that they had just been sent out.

"Who's in charge of this excursion?" Peter lashed out all of a sudden. "We want our money back."

A black man, obviously a Norcamtour representative, approached. Peter told him that since there were no seats available, they wanted a refund. Of course there were seats, said the black man and pointed at the narrow bench at the end of the bus.

"No," said Peter, "we won't sit there. My wife's health is not good. Give us our money back."

The black man begged them to understand the situation and be satisfied with the bench. Peter was stubbornly insistent. Finally the tourists in the bus started to change seats. In their hurry to leave, two seats were vacated. Instead of the bench, Peter and Sylvia were offered seats right above the back of the left wheel. While less comfortable than the bench, it didn't bother Peter. The main thing was he won.

On the way to the seats he shot a glance at the black woman who had chased them out.

"Does the lady consent to letting us ride in the same bus with her?" Peter said. It turned out that she was not a Norcamtour employee but a tourist. She stared at the seat in front of her without a word.

The bus set out.

Even before the two vehicles encroached upon the parched plain, the sky's oven was afire. Peter was fixed on a guidebook about Africa, Sylvia was observing the other passengers. Almost all of them were armed with movie cameras, photo cameras, light gauges, extra lenses, and piles of reserve film. A Tyrolean had a lens of such proportions that his camera looked like a cannon. Most of all, they were weighed down with plastic bottles of distilled water, which the driver packed between pieces of ice in a metal crate behind his seat. Peter and Sylvia had brought only one thermos into which they had poured some orange juice. The excursion organizer had surely been the one who provided the water in the crate.

They drove across the endless plain, along narrow, rutted paths, looking for animals. The sky was dark blue and cloudless and the sun was a formless source of blinding rays. The savanna inspired a feeling of piercing sadness in Sylvia. If the guide sitting next to the driver saw an animal, the bus would stop or come to a crawl. The windows opened and the barrels of the photography equipment pointed outside. Click-whir-cluck, it went: Kodak stockholders were getting richer by the minute. Sylvia didn't want to get her camera out, the animals were too far away, nothing would be visible in the pictures.

Sometimes the tourists could go out to see a flock of birds at a watering hole, a half-eaten antelope carcass, giraffes grazing amid the acacia trees, their ears above the crowns. Or a cluster of elephants showering and snorting in a muddy puddle. Then onward. And onward. Sometimes right through branches and grass, over cracked, parched earth. Kilometers of still emptiness, kilometers of discomfort, heat, and thirst stretched between stops.

The plastic bottles of water started to dwindle in the crate. The tourists' hot mouths drank and smacked as if taking a last swallow before death. The old French woman sitting with her husband in front of Peter and Sylvia looked around. When she saw they were already delirious from dehydration, she offered them a bottle with a kind smile. They mumbled their thanks breathlessly and passed it from mouth to mouth with trembling hands. Then they returned it to the lady. The ritual was repeated another five times. Whenever the French woman and her husband drank, Peter and Sylvia got a few sips, too.

Then Sylvia noticed that only some tourists were taking water from the crate. She also noticed the crosses, circles, and other marks on the bottles. Finally it flashed through her mind that the water wasn't for everyone, that the tourist agency hadn't provided it. It had only supplied the crate with ice; the tourists had brought their own water. Actually only a few had brought it, those who knew what awaited them. The Frenchwoman, God knows why, was giving them her own water. After Peter's crude clamor, the Frenchwoman's concern for Sylvia deeply moved her. She couldn't imagine what she would have done without those sips. She probably would have suffered heatstroke. Five hours after arriving at the park, they were still circling the white-hot plain looking for signs of life.

They stopped at a watering hole. The water had evaporated. Half-gelled, sticky mud covered the bottom. Birds that had mistakenly touched its surface got stuck and, unable to fly off, were slowly dying. The scene brought forth a strong recollection of something familiar, but Sylvia couldn't decide what. A hyena ran by. The sense of the magical presence of God knows what persisted. And it grew stronger when they met a lone hunter who had just caught a small monkey. Holding it by the skin of its neck, he pointed west. He had seen some lions there. The tourists returned to the bus one by one and they drove westward.

Peter, who still preferred to read a book than look out at the savanna, said, "Here it says that a lion will never attack a white man if he can get a black man. Most often he will avoid humans and chase a zebra. Zebras have more meat and don't shoot."

They finally caught sight of them. Four beasts were breathing heavily in the shade of some bushes. They were so haggard and sleepy, they would have inspired more fear had they been stuffed.

King of the Jungle? Sylvia marveled. The lion, which she had seen at the zoo a year ago might have deserved such an appellation, but here in its habitat the maned cats resembled unwashed, unkempt elders. They dozed, muzzles on their front paws, completely immobile. Only occasionally did one twitch its tail. Once in a while one of the males raised his eyelids and directed an uninterested look at the bus. At her, it seemed to Sylvia. Maybe the lack of interest was just concealed caution. It was possible that in a moment of danger the flaccid flesh would compress into a mass of muscles and spring to action.

The guide said that water was trucked in to fill the watering holes, but it evaporated immediately. There weren't enough trucks, so the animals were getting weak and dying off. Whole herds of elephants had moved away. And it was possible that drought wasn't the only thing killing the animals in Waza. People were whispering that the trucks that brought water by day took out crates of elephant tusks under cover of night.

"Listen to this," said Peter. Amazingly, the animals in the shade of the bushes didn't interest him in the least because he kept paging through the book. "Here it says that every so many years there appears a lion that likes only human flesh . . . "

Maybe one ought to appear more often, thought Sylvia, and chased Peter's voice from her mind. They drove on. On the plain in the national park that stretched from Cameroon into Chad and Nigeria, they came upon only two herds of elephants. And some giraffes, a few lions. Two antelopes. And some ravens. And a hyena. She had seen more animals at home, at the zoo.

Late in the afternoon they stopped at yet another dried-up puddle. Something attracted the guide's attention. Sylvia opened the window, leaned out, and exclaimed, "Oh, look!" A lion cub was lying in the dry grass. It had a broken leg and was starved almost to death; flies were feeding on the open wound on its back. Yet there was not a trace of fear in its eyes. This time there was no doubt: its eyes were focused on Sylvia. Maybe the cub was attracted by her cry or unexpected movement as she leaned out the window, almost as if it had noticed something precious, close, something it had been missing.

Then Sylvia roughly pushed Peter's knees aside and jumped into the aisle. She hurried to the bus door. On the way, she snatched the plastic bottle from the Frenchwoman's hands and another from the crate which still carried some water.

"No, miss, it's dangerous!" screamed the guide, but it was too late. Sylvia had already thrust the door open, falling more than stepping onto the ground. She ran around the bus. Then she slowed her steps to cautious, almost catlike movements as she approached the wounded wild cat. Despite its youth, it was almost as large as she was. As if unaware of what she was doing, she dropped to her knees beside it. She uncapped the bottle and poured a little water into her cupped palm. The thirsty lion cub gratefully lapped the water.

Then it put its head down on Sylvia's lap, as if it wanted to rest on something soft and safe.

The scene sent the tourists in the bus into a frenzy of snapping and shooting; no one wanted to miss the opportunity to embellish his family album with an image of harmony, almost trust, almost mutual comfort between two worlds, between instincts and feelings, between shared suffering and human mercy, which shone on Sylvia's suddenly beautiful, blessed face as an ethereal illumination.

Peter succumbed, too. For the first time since they reached the preserve, he pulled his automatic Pentax out and aimed it at his wife. Through the lens, she looked into his soul more rebelliously than in all the years he had domesticated and trained her like a compliant house pet. Her look told him that she had escaped from the home he had taken pains to build and fence so they would both be safe. She had escaped into a world he didn't understand, back to the savanna, the heat, the solitude, the inaudible wind.

Dress Rehearsal, II

• CHRISTINE HAMM •

You slip her on the bed, I remove her shoes. The sun flows wetly through the room, a sodden yellow orange. A high whining, dragonflies in the rafters. Through the window, we watch the trees turn dark and disappear. She breathes slowly next to us. I get a washcloth, warm it with hot water in the sink and dab at her face. You tell me I am turning into her as you try on her hat. We sit on the edge of the bed and watch *Gilligan's Island*, narrating the wardrobe choices so she can hear.

The Body and the Damage Done
• CHRISTINE HAMM •

You keep all our dead dears in the freezer: Mother's crown of violets, the mouse you named after a month, the seagull chick I tried to feed in secret. I wish I could stop loving her skeleton—she pushes so insistently, twisting my fingers, taking my heart into her dead mouth but refusing to bite.

You must have some hope at the end, my doctor tells me, *otherwise, no one will want to read you.* Before I met you, I met a man who was scarred on the inside of his thighs, as if torn by a woman's metal nails. He never told me the story of what happened to him. He tore at me when I was sleeping—I woke up on the steps of a subway station, sheets wrapped around me.

Glitter

• ROSE HUNTER •

One night the guy in the downstairs apartment, D., whose random screams I'd been listening to for days, cut his wrists and took a bunch of pills. Then he knocked on my door.

"Are you serious?" I yelled, when he told me what he'd done.

I waited until I heard him putter away and then opened the door. Red splats decorated the stoop. I peered over the balcony and saw him sitting on the stairs, clutching a bloody towel.

"Call A.," he yelled. "I've tried to kill myself!"

A. was our landlord. I called his number but there was no answer. Then I went downstairs. I'd been kicking back in front of the TV with a few vodka sodas, and the warm night air had a fuzzy, hazy quality.

D. put the towel next to him on the step and stared down at his wrists. The wounds were horizontal at least but jagged and gaping, like a Halloween pumpkin. I looked away. The smell of blood and tequila wafted up.

I got a towel from my apartment and wrapped his wrists, tucking the ends under. I couldn't think of anything to fasten them with. Bright red seeped through the white fabric.

"Stay still," I said. "I'm calling the ambulance."

"I've taken twenty clonazepam as well," he said. "These, there." He nodded at the crushed packet lying in front of his door. His small, desperate eyes shone proudly.

"Well," I said. "You'll probably be all right with that. I did the same thing the other week, *mas o menos*. With half a liter of vodka."

He stared at me. I shrugged. The reasons for this incident on my part were complex and not anything I was planning, at that stage, to examine.

D. pulled at the towels with his teeth. Overall there was a pinched quality to his face; an entrenched aspect of complaint.

I didn't know the number for the ambulance and didn't have a phone book so I called my ex-boyfriend, also a D.—and also three sheets to the wind, as usual.

"Uh, try 060," he slurred. "That's general emergency."

In my broken Spanish, I struggled to relate the situation to the operator, along with my address, which is not on a street with a name, but off a cobblestone road and up some stairs and then up a pedestrian-only alleyway. It took a while, but I got through it.

When I finished the towels were lying on the step. D. was holding his wrists up, examining them. Then he started screaming.

"Arghhh! Ahhhhhhh!"

A light flicked on in the apartment opposite mine, upstairs. The guy who lived there was standing at the window. I waved at him and he turned around. Seconds later the light in the apartment went back off.

"I'm such a loser," D. wailed. "I've lost everything. My daughter, my wife, my job . . . I can't work anymore."

"Okay, keep still."

"I was in the film industry in L.A. I worked with Mariah *Carey* . . . But now I can't go back there. I've lost it all. I'm such a *loser*. Arggh!"

"Ahhhhhhhh . . . "

He got up and trotted into his apartment. I followed and watched as he rifled through some stuff on the kitchen counter. Blood dripped onto the concrete floor, and onto a yellow plastic bottle, Tonayán—the cheapest brand of tequila.

"Look. She's in here."

I glanced at what he was foisting at me: a leather-bound photo album, scuffed around the edges. It was full of famous people, he said. The only one I recognized was Mariah Carey—her head cocked to one side, doe eyes flirting with the camera.

"She always shows the right side of her face huh, in photographs?" I said. "I read that somewhere. She thinks it's her better side."

In Mariah's hair was a sparkly clip in the shape of a large bird.

"What is that," I leaned forward to get a better look. "An ostrich?"

"I worked on one of her movies."

He gazed at me, an anguished look on his face.

"Movies? What movies?"

"*Glitter.*"

"Oh."

"I used to work with all of them. Look!"

He kept flipping through the album.

"I had a great life!"

"Well—that's good."

"But I've lost it all!"

He flung one arm over his head.

"Okay, why don't you settle down. Here, let me put these towels back on."

"I can't go back to the States."

"There we go."

He sat down on the floor, clutching the photo album to his chest.

"I've got three DUIs. They won't let me go back."

"Well then," I said. "Puerto Vallarta's not so bad is it?"

"I'm from Calgary. But I don't want to go back there. I want to go back to L.A. My wife and daughter are there. Look."

He opened the photo album again. "Oh, they must be in the other. Aaahhhh . . . "

"I've lost them!"

He squinted up at me. "I took *twenty* of those pills. I wonder what will *happen.*"

"You're used to them to some extent I'm guessing? Probably you'll just be very relaxed for a few days."

"I took *twenty* . . . "

"Look, you don't have to believe me. The doctor's coming. No, no, keep the towels."

"It's because I screw everything up! It's terrible."

He went into it further: all the things lost. Houses, cars, family. Eventually I heard a walkie-talkie and went to the door, looked out. Three police officers in white uniforms appeared out of the darkness, up the hill.

"*Suicidio, intento,*" I told them. "Ugh. *Las manos.*" I pointed to what was self-evident and showed them the empty pack of clonazepam as well. The first officer glanced at it and looked D. up and down with no change in his expression.

"Is he your husband?" he asked me, in English.

"No!" I shrieked. "I mean no. I live upstairs. This is the first time I've spoken to him. He knocked on my door."

"Okay." The officer took a few steps away and talked on his phone. Then he sauntered back.

"How old are you?" he asked D.

"Forty-three."

"Forty-three," the officer repeated, looking bored. "And why do you want to do this? Life is not so bad."

The other two officers wandered around the apartment, peering in D.'s closet and lifting up the odd dish. One of them kicked at the other plastic tequila bottles littering the floor and smirked. Then they both stood by the door, staring out over the alley.

D. picked up his photo album and showed the first officer the picture of Mariah Carey. He frowned and then a look of recognition came over his face and he nodded. He motioned to the other officers to look as well. They started talking, pointing at the picture and laughing. Then the first officer snapped the album shut. The other two drifted back to the door.

"I worked with her on *Glitter*," D. said. "It was a movie—*Glitter.*"

The officer shrugged.

After a while a guy in a red *Bomberos* shirt showed up. He was wearing a headband with a light attached to it, and he peered into D's eyes.

The officer asked for identification and D. started rifling around in a black case. I took this opportunity to slink back to my apartment. I hadn't been in the country long but my ex had instilled it in me that it was a good idea to make oneself scarce any time official documents were being requested, of anyone.

"Those pills will kick in," was the last thing I heard D. shout. "I took twenty of them! Yes, yes!"

I locked my door and lay down in the dark.

Gun Powder

• SHALOM MENSU IKHENA •

I was 16 the first time I met Yemi. Yemi with the inquisitive eyes and few words. He was a delicious kind of mystery and our relationship felt like a collection of medals.

The first medal I achieved was getting him to talk about his past for the first time. I was eager to hear the source point of his enigma. Yemi's dad name was Ade. Ade: head of the hunting clan; he that no one crosses, the lion whose back never meets the floor. His name meant crown; such a fitting name to a dominating character.

That was all I knew about his father, a hardly revealing picture of his spirit. I was left to fill in the physical features.

I earned the second medal from the first time he held my hand. The first time I had ever felt his skin. His hands were rough and firm, unusually intimate and almost afraid to let go. I often imagine what mine felt like against his, probably sweaty from the firmness of his grip.

He gave me the third medal, my favorite medal of all. It was after one of his hunting trips. He had ran to my place, eyes glowing with pride. I had never seen Yemi with an excess of any emotion. His already broad chest seemed broader, he looked taller. He was swelling before me. He had shot his first lion. I previously had heard of his many failed trials to kill one. It was his father's greatest achievement, seven lions victim to his wrath, a number not previously achieved in a lifetime. His father's name was spread across the village and neighboring villages like wild fire.

There was something about the fact that he had come all the way to tell me of his capture; it lifted me. It was the kind of buoyancy that accompanies a wealth of importance. Maybe he felt the airiness as well because he looked at me with eyes half confused by its gloss and putting precious cowries in my hands, he said:

"Ewa, ewa bi oti, je kin to ju e titu lailai." *Beauty, your beauty is like alcohol, let me take care of you forever.*

Many medals later, we were married; Yemi and I. I often found myself cleaning up after my words, and on some days my mouth was filled with things to say, things that never overflowed but sat stale and desperate. Yemi was still a mystery, a now distant kind of puzzle with no solution.

Three years later, they had come to our village. Humans with skin like the hard inside of a coconut. Children were being sold for mirrors and guns smaller and faster than we had ever seen. I had not spoken to Yemi about them. He was the kind of person that avoided talking about life threatening situations. An interesting breed of cowardice: denial.

Yemi had come back especially late from his hunting trip today. His absence left me uneasy, I had reheated his meal 3 times already to fill the time. Time that refused to pass as though mocking my efforts to ignore its sluggishness.

"My husband. Where have you been? I have been awaiting your return." I said walking towards him hurriedly to assure myself that he had not been hurt.

"How do I provide food for this family? You know where I have been."

"I am sorry I asked, but you should come home earlier, there are men in this village looking for slaves. If they take you from me, how will I survive, who do I beg for your return?"

"Ikore, you worry like a child with pepper in his eye. Who will take me away? My gun will hit the man's chest before he sees the hem of my shirt. Forget about this, do you have my food prepared?"

"My people say it is only a coward that sees danger and closes his eye. Yemi, a word is enough for the wise."

I could see the change in his face with my last statement. God forbid I call Yemi a coward. His nose flared with anger and I could hear his breath quickening. I hoped he would finally talk about what was happening in the village or talk to me about anything at all but all he said was:

"Ikore, you dare look to my face and call me a coward? Oh, even a foolish woman knows not to bite the finger of the man that feeds her."

And with that he left for his room, refusing to eat his dinner.

Five days later, Yemi still had not uttered a word to me since our last argument. I was cooking his dinner I knew he would once again refuse when the coconut colored men arrived at our home. One of them held a bag of guns that weighed him down.

After I had realized I was being sold, it was a saddening kind of joke that my first thought was that there should have been more. That if he was going to sell something as valuable as our love, his return should have been one involving many men, carrying hefty bags, bags heavy enough to break the backs of warriors. I should have gone for more than one sickly bag of guns.

1.2.3.4.5

• SHALOM MENSU IKHENA •

Her skin was grey and scarred. Her eyes held liquid fear, or was it anger? Her gait was tired and feline, as though futile hope lay heavily on her waist. She was the newest slave girl but a divine dancer. She would dance for our ceremonies, waist adorned with the finest of beads, shoulders hidden in heavy ornaments. Her dance steps were slow and beckoning. How could an essence so strange carry such elegance on its shoulders? The stride of her hips, the expression on her face, spoke words she could never utter. The stamp of her feet against the soil would send dust particles up in the air like saluting soldiers. Her slight, almost beguiling smile would carry men on an unsatisfying journey.

I tried not to think about her often, but it was incredibly difficult. There are, sorry, there were five things about her. There were many things about her but I now remember five most vividly.

1. Her hair. Bouncy and resilient. A character in itself. A perfect completion to the masterpiece that was her face.
2. Her collarbone. The way it sunk with long drawn out laughter. I would often imagine kissing the space between them just to taste the vibration of her joy.
3. Her waist. Now, I am not one to see a woman as a collection of body parts, but oh lord, the wonder that was her waist. The magic it created when the drums started. I would watch her move and it would feel like the only reason my world spun was because it was her hula-hoop.
4. Her eyes. Poetry locked in eyelids. They were the kind that kept you up all night, wishing you could watch her sleep. If for nothing else, to witness her eyelids break open in the morning.

5. Her fingers. Long and slender. Uncannily delicate. I would watch her bathe master's children and I would long to know the feel of her palm. Bury my nose in the bliss of her skin.

And once in a while, in the heat of a dance, she would move in the direction of the crowd, a frenzy of vibrations taking over her waist and shoulders. A mix of pride and satisfaction would flash across her face. She was well aware of the empire she had created in our minds. One in which the slave became the dictator.

How does one fall in love with the slave girl he bought for his soon returning master?

Ladonia, Texas
1943

• FRANKLIN LAFAYETTE KING •

The lingering heat of August boldly drifted into September. Ladonia, Texas awaited the first dry norther of the fall. Loud cicadas clung to the cotton wood trees that wainscoted the oiled roads that led to the elementary school. Yellow jackets and dirt dobbers hummed in the heat of the classroom where Mr. Percy Yorktown, wilted by heat, attempted to teach.

Percy Yorktown, Ladonia's newly employed elementary school teacher, had decided to attend the nearby Normal school solely to avoid being drafted. He reasoned that if he became a schoolteacher, he would not be drafted or so he hoped. The local cemetery was already receiving the bodies of the farmers' sons that were not professional educators.

Drinking Early Times and occasional profanity were the outward manifestations of his manhood. He had neither drunk nor cursed before he pledged a fraternity in college. It was in his senior year before he stopped believing that the purposes of such an organization were the obtaining of high grades and protecting the chastity of women. It is quite possible that Percy was the only fraternity member that had actually practiced the idealized rites of his brotherhood. The fact that he was twenty-one and still a virgin bothered him.

"One more year of war has gone by, and I am still safe. Surely the conflict will end soon, and I can leave this asshole of a town and go to Dallas."

Gene's Hotel had withstood both time and marginal upkeep during its forty-seven years of operation. Its date of origin was plastered in large, bold script upon the front of the building as though its date of construction held some significance to its largely migratory guests. Prominently displayed in the lobby were oversized NO LOITERING and NO SPITTING signs that were easily read in the hotel's dim interior. As if to underscore the intent of the management to discourage loafing, the restrooms in the main lobby were pay toilets. Gene's was also the Greyhound, Trailway and Mooney bus station.

From the street, sweet potato vines could be seen growing out of tea colored water filtered behind screens patched with chewing gum. Gene's was a hotel without reputation, for the people who either stayed the night or lodged there permanently only had one thing in mind: Sleep.

Each of the three floors of rooms had its one single communal bathtub. The water for the bathtub was heated solely, at least the guest believed, by the blaze of the gas pilot light. Also shared by the tenants was a perpetual supply of Sweetheart Soap, one of the few free offerings of the hotel. Gene's was unique in that the towels bore not the name of the hotel but titles such as: Galves, Adolphus, White Plaza, and Jack Tar.

"Oh Lord, I can't believe that I live here," swept through Percy's mind as he entered the front screen with its ornate Grapette thermometer sign. The one interesting thing about Gene's was Mrs. Evans who was the proprietress. Not only did she tend the main desk but she also unloaded the buses and drove Ladonia's one taxi. Mrs. Evans had dyed blond hair and was very attractive for a lady in her early fifties.

"Hello, Mr. Percy, have a nice day at school?" Paula Evans said with a smile.

It was Percy's habit on a Friday night to go to the Fox Theater and view whatever was showing. The Fox had no matinee since the kids worked in the fields until dark. The first feature started at 8:00 p.m. and ran over and over until there was not an audience to be seen in the theater. No one, to Percy's knowledge, had ever witnessed the theater closing for nearly all of its patrons were asleep by ten even on a Saturday night.

The Fox was opened three nights a week. Thursday night was space night; Friday, cowboys, and Saturday was devoted to crime and on Sunday, which could have been the high water mark for the theater, even the Fox rested as the owners did not believe in working on Sundays.

The Friday night movie was *Montana Kid*. Percy carefully studied the displays outside, especially the coming attractions. While the Fox did not sell tickets until 7:50, the proprietress would set in the box office window from 7:00 until opening time, counting change. This was an irritation because the appearance of the box office "girl" should be a cue that the tickets were ready.

The mistress of the box office was in her late seventies, wore rhinestone jewelry and a fox stole with the nose of one fox shoved into the mouth of the adjoining one.

As she counted the money, her lips puckered in time with the stacking of the change. The aroma of freshly popped popcorn as well as the thought of a coke in a Dixie cup with crushed ice transfixed those waiting in line. The clientele were not trusted with bottles and were forced into either purchasing or slipping in their own soft drinks since the theater had no drinking fountains. The thought of that primary deprivation of human need immediately created thirst.

"Thank god," thought Percy when 7:50 finally arrived. He always felt foolish waiting with so many of his students for the Fox to open. He thoroughly disliked the other members of the audience. He went to the movies for escapism and isolation while the rest of Ladonia went to visit, laugh, snack on popcorn and eventually to sleep under the large fan. Frequently during a film, Percy could be seen changing his location from one section to another. How often he moved depended upon how irritated he had become.

Many of the poorer clientele brought their own unshelled pecans, cokes and candy with them. It was well known that the concession stand charged extra for everything. What particularly annoyed Percy was when a young lady named Venus showed up with her apples. Venus was a challenged learner and ate apples constantly during each film. One could easily locate her position in the theater by listening.

After the coming attractions and the ageless Chevrolet advertisement, the main feature would begin, and so did Venus with her first apple. The students talked and whistled at each other while the maiden voyage of a coke bottle rolled from the back of the theater to the front hitting metal stanchions on its journey to the screen.

No one but Percy seemed to be watching the movie. He soon began to change his seating position. First he located himself in front of the Black section. An older man started to snore. Obviously he had hoed cotton all day and the large fan, which cooled the theater, had provided the first opportunity to be comfortable and to eventually sleep. The snoring became louder and louder.

"Lord, god!" thought Percy. Then he shifted to the lower left hand corner of the theater. And yes, he could hear a loud crunch just behind him. Venus had started to munch her second apple. Percy then shifted to the middle of the theater and sat down on a Milky Way Bar that attempted to glue him to the protruding spring in the seat.

Percy immediately stood up and addressed the audience as though he were an actor in the film, "Damn you sons-of-bitches! Why in the hell can't you be quiet during a movie? You shit asses!" He then sat down and could feel his heart pounding.

It dawned on him that he had just addressed some of the leading citizens' children in Ladonia. Compounding his problem was that he was on the library censorship committee.

The theater was suddenly quiet but for Montana Kid's horse baying and some snickering at the back of the theater. Then a small mummer of conversations ensued. Percy felt a tap on his shoulder and a fox's nose on the back of his neck.

"Mr. Yorktown, I'm afraid that we don't allow obscenities at the Fox. I am going to have to report you to the head of the school board. After all, his daughter is in the theater, and you are her teacher. Shame on you!"

"Shit on your fox!" shouted Percy and with that comment he left the theater. A summer storm was entering Ladonia as he walked into the night.

Percy knew that his life had been unalterably changed. The Montana Kid had killed him as well as the outlaws in the film. No one would hire an obscene elementary school teacher. He was now in definite jeopardy of being drafted. Rather than riding into the sunset, he had inadvertently saddled his horse up for the war.

The Ask Sandwich

• LYNN LEVIN •

The TSA lady at Newark Airport had a nice touch, and Josie enjoyed the pat down. The blue gloves slid under her arms, along her sides, down one leg, then the other. They searched, discerned. They pleased with just the right amount of pressure. Josie thanked the TSA lady, who nodded back with very professional brown eyes.

In bed last night in Robert's apartment, it was their sixth time together, Josie had attempted the "ask sandwich," something she'd read about in a woman's magazine. First she told him how nice his cologne smelled and trailed her fingers playfully down his arm. That was the first slice of bread. Then she said she'd really love it if he rubbed her back. That was the sandwich filling. She would have praised him and reciprocated generously, which would have been the other slice of bread.

Instead he said, "You're really bossy, aren't you?"

Sheesh. She'd only done what the magazine had instructed. Josie curled away from Robert, then on his hard mattress, she recovered a little backbone. "I don't consider that so bossy."

"Well, I do." The atmosphere in the room wadded up like paper.

Pulling her carry-on bag, striding in beige pumps, Josie made her way to her gate. She tried to wall off the Robert fiasco and focus on the nursing conference in Atlanta. She was looking forward to presenting her paper on pressure sores but hoped her seatmate would not inquire about her work. She'd about had it with folks who squinted and scrunched their faces when she told them about her field. Oh, you mean bedsores, they'd say using the old term. Didn't know they were that important. Well, they can be fatal, she'd retort. She would educate them a little about patients who were stuck in bed, about reduced blood supply, friction, cell death, complications. And that pretty much ended the conversation.

At first, she'd seen a future with Robert. They agreed on politics and comedians, hated remakes of classic films, and pork pie hats.

Maybe she should try being old school, passive. What was she anyway, a thirty-three-year-old sensualist who only thought of touch? And she wasn't exactly a winner in the dating game—one six-month relationship and a lot of first dates with few follow-ups. Was it her or Match.com?

On the way to her gate, Josie passed a Hudson News. An array of cover girls beckoned her, fringed by come-on headlines: *Drive him wild tonight. Ten types of sex to try at least once. Better orgasms now.* Did everything have to be about the sack? Well, she would like to have some great sex before she died. Addicted to the promises on the cover, she bought a copy of *Cosmopolitan.*

Josie's seatmate was a fortyish man in a blue short-sleeved shirt and Phillies baseball cap who said his name was Solly.

Josie said her name was Mimi.

Solly smelled freshly showered and had a dimple in his chin. They chatted about the weather and airplane coffee. When he asked her what she did for a living, she told him she booked models for fashion ads. With a light heart, she fibbed her way through a conversation about beauty, dieting, and divas. She'd met the famous Kate Upton. Yes, Karlie Kloss really was that skinny.

Solly said he didn't know who those women were, but he complimented Josie on her big career.

"Sometimes those girls are so beautiful and sexy they're unreal," said Josie.

"I like the real type," said Solly with a playful grin. "Real gals, like you." As he sipped his airplane coffee, Josie spied no wedding ring. The two laughed a lot. Each time she said something he found fetching, he touched her shoulder. He had a big paw, but his touch was gentle and warm. It would have been nice to get to know him better. When it turned out they were both from central Jersey, Solly asked if he could have her phone number. Could he call her sometime?

This Josie now desperately wanted, but her wardrobe of lies made it impossible. She gulped and rubbed her nose. She almost knocked her coffee off the little depression in her tray table. "I guess with your schedule that would be hard to arrange," he said.

"I do travel a lot," said Josie reluctantly.

Solly opened his laptop and began to study some documents. Josie paged through her *Cosmo*. Her head felt hot. She was very cross with herself, whoever she was.

Bulldog

• PAUL LISICKY •

The bulldog kept the woman alive, but the woman didn't know that. She had other problems on her mind, such as where did she put her keys, and what was her car doing in Florida when she'd parked it in Tennessee?

The bulldog got very still when the woman started shoving her fingers into the dishes and the bowls. He figured he could make the earth spin a little slower if he were sitting on its axis, so he'd quiet his panting; he'd look straight ahead, neither left nor right. The woman would trip on him, wince at him for being in her way, then lean down and palm the top of his head, thus assuring him they were in their correct positions to one another, and they'd get through one more day.

After she loaded the dishes in the dishwasher, the woman headed to her recliner every night. It was always a bit of a production. First the blanket went over the legs, then the cushion went behind her neck, and once she settled in, the bulldog commenced his stunning leap and landed in her lap. The woman always told herself she was watching her favorite program, but she was inevitably sound asleep before the first commercial. And inside the warm nest of the lap, the bulldog began his work, which was to calm the woman while the woman dreamt of lost things. It took great work to be her purifying organ, but he always felt better when he did so. It gave him the illusion of aliveness even if it made him tremble, even if he had to play dumb and weak in order to get the tenderness he craved.

What was the woman thinking when she looked at him as if he were an intruder? Her eyes went wild that day; her hands flew up. But there was a quiet in her too that took away any desire he had to speak. He didn't go out to pee as he usually did but let go right there on the rug, by the umbrella stand. And when he tried to leap on the woman's lap, his nails snagged in her afghan. Gone was her old face of curiosity and concern. In its place was something more remote. Her face might have been made of granite, which wouldn't have been so bad if granite hadn't smiled.

When the woman could no longer tell the difference between the phone and the channel changer, the woman faced the front door. She stood there a few minutes more before she was guided by two strangers to a car outside. How new she looked to the bulldog. Though she could barely put one foot in front of the next, she might have been walking into the world for the very first time, learning to make it through a day all over again. And in taking that in, the bulldog's face went completely white in an instant, as if someone had taken a match to it.

He never saw the woman's face again. The apartment grew dirty, he took to whatever was left in the cabinets: raisins, mice, the bristles of an old brush. It might have been years, it might have been days. And when he grew tired of living the life of the saint, he squeaked out through a crack of light beside the door, and lived longer than he'd ever thought.

Beachtown
• PAUL LISICKY •

The birds can go elsewhere. The maritime forest? Let it burn to the ground. The palms along the causeway can go up with it. The spiders, the fleas, the rats, the snakes: any living creature that lives in the leaves. They can burn up too. Ruby thinks these thoughts while she volunteers at the beach town bird sanctuary, dispensing wisdom to the schoolchildren bused in from the mainland. They all think she's a nice lady in her aqua sundress and her benign smiling face. The wrens who eat nuts and seeds out of her hand think she's a nice lady too. Is she a nice lady? She wonders whether she doesn't think enough about that question. She thinks a lot about her house in the woods, the house with the anchor patterns on the shutters, the house she's lived in since childhood. She thinks a lot about selling it to a rich young couple who will surely destroy it. She'll watch the bulldozer ramming the sun room where her mother once poured cereal. She'll look at the accomplishment and indifference on the young couples' faces, then she'll drive back to the new condo she's bought on the mainland, with its granite and stainless steel and cobblestone drive—every amenity she despises. Isn't that what they call them these days? Amenities?

There is an awful chorus of horns one morning. The black snake with the pink spots is once again sunning itself in the road. It is the same snake that has scared the neighborhood senseless for the past week. Ruby feels friendly to the snake. She is a great appreciator of the way it has frightened the children, making them cower inside their houses, in front of their laptops and gameboys at night. Ruby leaves it a dish of milk by the front door before she goes to sleep, and when it is morning, it is almost empty, with only a few drops left. It makes her happy that the snake is drinking her milk. Maybe she will go on-line some night to find out what a good snake eats.

Now the new couple next door is out waving their arms over their heads. They are blurred with fury. They are shouting at the driver of the Land Rover, with his righteous, twisted face behind glass. He wants to go forward. The snake is as still as a question mark. It will not move, and the car is full of passengers who are hungry. They will not be stopped for one more minute. The young couple cannot stand that there are people like the passengers of the Land Rover in the world. The way they plead and cajole, you might think the neighborhood has always been just for them, built in anticipation of their arrival. The horn hurts Ruby's ears. It cuts right through the center of her. And for just this reason alone, Ruby rushes out the front door in her nightie and grabs the snake. The snake is cool and luscious in her hands. The palms go silent. The horn goes silent. The snake hunches left, right, it turns its face directly toward Ruby's face. It is asking her a question. It wants something of her. Yes, I know what you are, Ruby answers, though she holds those words in her head instead of speaking them. And just as the snake seems to close its eyes and sigh and shrink into itself in delirious pleasure, it lunges forward and jabs Ruby in the breast. Ruby moistens her bottom lip. The young couple is too shocked to scream. And just as Ruby begins to take in the clean sharp cut of the bite, the glistening needles of it, the snake goes back in a second time, and the purification she didn't know she'd been seeking begins to have its way with her.

Ugliest Child in America
• PAUL LISICKY •

In his 43rd year, Darren became a handsome man. Men and women grinned in his direction. Shopkeepers fussed over him, practically thanking him for not buying their goods. Strangers asked his opinion. Should cactus be planted in a yard where children play? Or: do you prefer bay swimming to ocean swimming? Darren took to his new position with a humility that made him even more endearing. He'd been the ugliest child in America—at least his grade school classmates had thought of him that way—and he knew the cost of donkey ears, a lantern jaw, and a black brow that met over his nose. At some point in human history it had been determined that beauty wasn't required of men, but people who thought like that hadn't met the Darren of old. They hadn't known what it was like to turn your light so low that no one could even see you walking down the street, lest they say something cruel, with a knife in it.

A Walking Stick with the face of a mule. That was what Darren heard behind his back one day.

A baboon without any of the lovely colors on his butt. He'd heard that one too.

Who knew that Darren had been born to be a 43-year-old man? If he had known that sooner, he would have spent his youth differently. He would have been helping the poor. He would have been lifting plastic from the estuaries instead of putting all that energy into transforming himself into a ghost.

One Friday night, Darren walked down the street to his cousin's bachelor party. His beard was trimmed. He had on the blue Oxford shirt and the pink bow tie. It pleased him to be the kind of man who could wear a pink bow tie. And as he smiled at the men and women walking by, he saw a younger man walking toward him with the lowest hairline he'd ever seen.

It wasn't just the hairline, but his lips, which were shiny and swollen, like some facial enhancement surgery gone awry. Darren heard himself think, *ugliest child in America,* and just as he was about to acknowledge the man with his gaze, to tell him, without words, *it isn't always going to be like this,* he felt something wet whip him in the eye. The younger man had flung some liquid from a vial, and as Darren felt his eyebrow, he recognized the smell as one of the household solvents of his youth. Okay, Darren thought, it's not acid. This will not destroy me. I am loved—somewhere. He heard the people crying around him. He imagined hands flying up to mouths, but he felt calm in the way that all injured animals feel calm. He was calm when the ambulance pulled up to the curb. He was calm even when the doctors told him that he'd lose sight in his left eye, and the iris would be permanently contracted, drifting around his cornea like a stray planet.

His eyes, his green eyes. Did it bother Darren that he wouldn't see from that eye? Not as much as his return to the Darren of old.

He wouldn't be a lion anymore.

He was in the coffee shop years later. He'd been running around the dog beach with his new dog, Josefa, and the little dog, who looked more like a little pig, had given more joy than he'd known in years. He was his feeling his luck again. He felt it in his chest, and in his calves, which were as plump as a mountain biker's. A small girl in pigtails stepped up to the counter with her father. She looked up at the bright blue fixtures on the ceiling, then set her eyes on Darren. Sweet, thought Darren. Pretty face. Instantly she buried herself into the fabric of her father's shirt. What's the matter, tulip? the father said, with tightened mouth. Monster, said the girl, pointing up at Darren. Monster. Get him out of here!

Darren did get out of there, to the dread of the father, who seemed to want to shake the girl, if not for himself, but for Darren. He walked out without picking up his coffee. Out on the sidewalk, under the awning, he put his finger to his eye. He actually touched the cornea, as if it were still possible to drag the iris to the center, as dumb as he knew that gesture to be. He did it once again, without flinching this time. A nun hobbled by with her cane, and then he recovered himself. There was the little dog at his feet, leashed to the bench. And when he leaned down to touch her, she let out a funny yap, as if to remind him she could have cared less about some stupid eye, having grown up with a missing ear and an irrepressible need to run.

Modernism
• PAUL LISICKY •

SPEEDBOAT
After Morris Lapidus' rendering of the International Trade Center

The speedboat I'm in barely makes a wake. The captain keeps his clothes on. I don't mind standing beside him in this swimsuit, because your eye goes only to the finger that's pointing ahead. It was never about the buildings, though they're as shapely as dresses. It was never about the plants and flags: they're only in the way. It's what you can't see that makes you want it, which is why you're relieved the dream stays just a dream. Isn't it better that the bay we're passing through never burns our nostrils with oil, never uglies our drinking supply, never rises higher than the seawall, slopping the parks and lights and trees? Just a blue, tranquil mirror intended to lengthen and stretch. Everything poised on becoming, which is where we always wanted to be. And though the palm beside us looks like it might murder us—Look! Three times taller than the towers in the distance!—what it wants of us is wonder: to empty us out that we might start all over again.

TEARDOWN

When the woman at the fancy dinner dismissed the populist modernist houses that he so loved, she probably didn't know that she was committing murder. But if she did know, she did it with maximum efficiency, as if by taking down the glass walls, the posts and beams, the leafy atriums, she was dismantling everything they stood up against: darkness, meanness, the small constricted ways of the past. And just when he thought he couldn't stand it anymore, she let him know with a subtle smile that her sister had demolished

79

one of those same houses to build a monster house--not that she called it that—to the consternation of her neighbors on the street.

A Little Murder

Years before my teenage brother had collected enough mid-century modern furniture to fill up a three-bedroom summerhouse and then some, he bought a small teak figure resembling a Nordic explorer. He was twelve then. It wasn't long before he'd outgrown such simple taste and advanced to the next level, sophistication the order of the day: McCobb, Bertoia, Eames, Finn Juhl. As if to prove this to my mother and me, he held the little man in the air, daring us to stop him. His smile pulled in four directions at once: part triumph, part despair, part relief, part hatred. But in spite of our cries, he slammed the man against the wall. And when that didn't do it, he slammed it once again. We watched in awe as the head broke off, the shiny wooden torso rolling to the corner of the room. The house went quiet. Outside, beside the dock, an egret gave a little laugh. How could we be connected to something so spoiled and sick? What was ahead for us? We couldn't yet see that he needed to get it first before it got him, which is the way we are with perfection.

Coming Back to Earth as a Dog
• BOBBI LURIE •

Even after he shot me, I still loved him and even after I was dead I wanted to be with him. So I forgave him once more and made the crucial decision to come back to earth as a dog.

I say "earth" instead of "life" because life really is eternal; earth is just a dull and rather frightening universal halfway house for the immature and uncertain. Yet I always enjoyed life on earth. I liked the way the weather changed from sun to rain and back again. I liked the way the hedge along our front walkway got overgrown and how the abundant weeds threatened the life of my roses.

And I loved my life with Martin, in spite of our violent arguments. He never beat me, understand, but we had a gun in the house and often threatened to use it on each other. Unfortunately, on March the second, 1989 at 2:18 p.m., Martin went so far as to pull that trigger. My last sensations were of the sharp heat of the bullet and then the warm ooze of blood which swiftly carried me away from earthly consciousness. I felt as though I were waking from a dream and I found myself sinking deep into long-forgotten yet familiar territory.

Death was a magnificent release for me. There was no need for me to control anything anymore and I felt completely safe. I wanted to laugh at all the things that seemed so urgent and important to me on earth. Things like auditions and acting jobs and wrinkles forming at the corners of my eyes and hair turning gray and the rent which needed paying and my beloved collection of silver teaspoons I had collected from my travels around the world. I really made a fuss over this collection. In fact, it was over this very collection that I lost my life. I was furious at Martin for breaking the wooden shoe off the top of my delicately engraved windmill spoon from Holland. He had been using the spoon to repot his cereus peruvianus plant. My blinding rage led me to impulsively pick up a butcher knife, which led Martin to reach for the gun. I was still angry with him when my body hit the floor. He knew how much those little teaspoons meant to me and he knew they were only to be used for stirring milk and sugar into tea.

Martin and I made tea drinking into a type of ceremony. I'd lay my powder-blue tablecloth on the kitchen table and set out my special china cups, the sugar and the milk. My spoon collection would go in the center of the table and we'd both carefully select our spoon for the day. Martin's favorite spoon had the word INDIA engraved on the top of the spoon, which was carved in the shape of the Indian subcontinent. I was particularly fond of the spoons I collected in Eastern Europe but my favorite had always been that wooden shoe spoon from Holland.

We enjoyed our tea time when one of us was working and even better if we both had parts in a play or even a television commercial, but the long stretches of mutual unemployment had a negative effect on our relationship. We tended to blame each other for our bad luck. Martin's violent outbursts towards me were balanced by his heartfelt apologies. He'd often leave me for hours or even days on end, but then return with a bouquet of flowers or bottle of brandy. Sometimes he'd stay in the house with me after breaking a vase or throwing a pot against the wall; he'd kneel at my feet with his head in my lap crying, begging my forgiveness and telling me those eternally famous lies lovers tell, things like he loved me and couldn't live without me. He was an excellent actor so I'd enjoy these performances and never failed to forgive him in the 15 years we were together.

But on the afternoon of March 2, 1989 there wasn't much I could do. The blood was oozing out of my gut as I looked on helplessly at my lifeless complexion and grotesquely open mouth. The mess that death makes of a person is really embarrassing but Martin was kind enough to clean me up and once he realized I was truly dead he dug a deep hole beneath the plum tree in back of our house and buried me there.

To be honest, I hardly thought of Martin the first few years after my death. I was living in a sort of liquid consciousness, alone yet with the sense of being completely supported, held and loved. But time flies when you're in a state of bliss and I realized my life on this particular plane was about to end. No one told me this, of course, but I was certain of these facts since I existed in a realm where everything was understood. I knew I was free to either pass into eternity, enter another universe or return to earth for another expedition. Well, I've always loved to travel, even to the most godforsaken places, and it was hard for me to resist another expedition to earth.

It was clear to me that I didn't want to return to earth as a woman nor did I want to come back as a man. I did not miss all the ups and downs of human existence. But I wanted to be with Martin again and that's how I decided to come back as a dog. He always loved animals and especially dogs and I knew I could enter his life that way.

The plan was executed without a plan being made. I was born from the body of a dog who lived a few miles down the road from Martin. Her "owner" (humans somehow feel they "own" other creatures) was a little boy who delivered the Sunday paper. It seemed I was back into a body, this time a puppy's body, almost as soon as I decided to be. Until then I had forgotten what it was like to feel the crushing claustrophobia of physical pain. I regretted my decision to return to earth as soon as I felt myself being squeezed out of the tiny birth canal. It wasn't just the pain; it was also being surrounded by four other puppies and suddenly feeling myself to be separate from all of them.

I was in a terrified daze after the birth but my mother, who I once thought of as a mangy bitch, lured me to her with the sweetness of her breasts. After a communal meal with my brothers and sisters I would doze off to sleep with the comforting scent of my mother's fur entering my nostrils. I quickly realized that this earth was different than the one I knew as a human. As my eyes began to focus, I saw a world which was colored in a rather blurry haze. I was bombarded with sounds more three-dimensional than my vision. My delight came mostly through my incredible sense of smell, which made my body feel almost transparent.

The time with my canine mother ended one day when the boy, with a scent of dry blandness, lifted me and my brothers and sisters away from our mother's breast and tossed us into a putrid-smelling basket. We all cried out but he took no notice. He took us from house to house and one by one my brothers and sisters were picked out of the basket screaming their hearts out until I was left in the basket alone.

There was a shock of recognition when we arrived at Martin's house.

It was completely altered as I saw it in its faded blurriness, looking bigger, foggier and darker. The strong aroma of flowers and mud and birds and rotting wood turned this into a new universe, one which frightened me.

I saw a changed Martin, one large and colorless with blurred features and bent head, come to the large front door. He and the boy were saying something I could not understand. Martin smelled of sickness and sadness and his voice was deep and muddy. The closeness of his soft checkered shirt put me into a panic. Then I felt his hands reach around my trembling body. His fingers' long boniness brought me back to an old familiarity. It was like the times after a big fight when he would put his head on my lap and tell me he loved me and could not live without me.

Stalking Marcel Duchamp
• BOBBI LURIE •

I caught sight of him . . .

I was slipping on ice as I tried to keep hidden. I didn't want Duchamp to see me as the type of woman who would follow a dead man through a blizzard.

I justified my stalking by pledging to finally stop making art. If Marcel Duchamp could do it, I could do it too. I would give up art. Leave the scene. Without a trace. And Duchamp would teach me how.

The blizzard was gaining strength.

• • •

I saw Marcel Duchamp walk into an Italian restaurant on West Fourteenth Street.

I followed him and looked at him surreptitiously through the window.

I was perplexed.

Now that he was dead, I assumed Marcel Duchamp required nothing in the way of sustenance from this earth. But Marcel Duchamp was eating eagerly . . . between puffs on his cigar . . .

No one in America is allowed to smoke indoors . . . was this a dream?

I watched Duchamp eat . . . at the rate he was going, I figured it would take him less than fifteen minutes to finish his dinner.

Watching Duchamp, smoking freely in the restaurant, I suddenly longed for a cigarette. I bought a pack at *The Korean Market* next door. I lit match after match . . . but the wind was too strong.

A waiter walked out. He offered me a light. I accepted, dragging deep as he asked me what I was doing out in the blizzard. "I'm waiting for that guy," I said, pointing to my hero.

"Come in," he said, grabbing my arm, saving me from slipping on the ice.

I crushed the cigarette butt into the pavement, then picked it up and deposited it in the trashcan. I felt the waiter's impatience; he was pulling on my arm . . .

The waiter took me straight to Duchamp's table. Duchamp didn't seem to mind; he was smoking and drinking red wine . . .

I was mesmerized in Duchamp's presence. I stood there, amazed to be gazing at his hands, his face . . .

I looked down at his food: plain spaghetti with a pat of butter, grated Parmesan cheese over the pasta, a small glass of red wine . . . espresso after.

When the espresso came, Marcel Duchamp pointed to the coffee. And yes, I did agree with him: *everything is tautology except black coffee.*

When he was finished with his espresso, he lit a new cigar and motioned me to sit.

I did.

• • •

If this is a lucid dream, I told myself, *I'll direct myself to Paris, the Paris I could never find in Paris. I'll take Marcel with me.*

• • •

Marcel Duchamp blew smoke in my face, bringing my focus back to him.

He stood up slowly and started to walk ahead of me.

I was afraid I'd never see him again. Thinking quickly, I asked him if he'd like to go with me to The Museum of Modern Art for an opening that night.

"I have a horror of openings. Exhibitions are frightful . . . "

I stared into his green-striped, pink shirt.

After some moments of silence, he asked me if I'd like to see his apartment.

I didn't say a word; he knew I would . . .

• • •

I followed Marcel up five flights of dusty stairs. When we got to the landing, Marcel turned to me and said, "my intention was always to get away from myself . . . "

He unlocked the door of his apartment, held the door open wide, and motioned me in.

• • •

Marcel Duchamp's apartment was a mess. Clothes were spilling out of open drawers, onto the floor, a floor covered in dust which seemed to be inches thick, shoes and pillows were strewn across the room . . .

And yet . . .

A shiny porcelain urinal was hung over the doorway. Marcel Duchamp's snow shovel, suspended from the ceiling. His coat rack in the middle of the room, nailed to the floor.

I wanted to see more.

But a knock came to the door. The knock was insistent. It was his neighbor, a French lady with a powerful temper. Only later did I learn her name was Gisele.

Gisele's presence gave me a chance to take some moments to observe the disaster of Marcel's apartment. There was nothing which seemed congruent to my previous art historical exuberance. In any event, it was far more interesting watching Marcel and Gisele gesticulate in French.

Marcel Duchamp turned to me, explaining he needed to go upstairs with Gisele.

He asked me to follow.

I followed Marcel and Gisele up another two flights of stairs. A door was open. Water was seeping out, into the hallway, out to the stairs . . . Gisele motioned us into the apartment . . . I stepped into water . . . up to my ankles . . . uncomfortable in my own skin . . . the television set was on. Marcel Duchamp pointed excitedly to Lena Dunham having awkward sex with Adam Driver.

"Amusing," said Duchamp.

He stared into the screen, seemingly mesmerized. He laughed.

Girls reminded Marcel Duchamp of his painting, *Nude Descending a Staircase, No. 2.* "My aim was static representation of movement," he said,

"... the idea of describing ... movement of a nude ... retaining static."

"Yes," I said, "most viewers seem to be fascinated by her nudity," I wanted to say something more original so I added, "Lena Dunham has a unique way of showing friendships as hotbeds of betrayal."

... Marcel Duchamp looked down at his hands ...

When he finally looked up, he stared out into the distance.

His skin was a paler shade of gray. He turned to look at me, with new intensity.

"I'm tired ... even of existing," he said.

Then he looked away.

When he finally spoke again, he said, "Andre Breton ... can't be approached. He's playing the great man too much ... I don't dare telephone him anymore, it's ridiculous ... I'm ten years older than he is. I think I have a right to expect to hear from him, a telephone call, something."

Marcel Duchamp looked back at the television screen.

"... artists ... are limited," he said. "Masturbation is what it is."

• • •

The water was rising.

Gisele walked up to Marcel, her face touching his.

Marcel Duchamp remained calm in spite of her fury. In fact, he looked happy.

He turned to me, took my hands and excused himself with some words of courtesy; he explained that he had promised to fix Gisele's toilet; he asked if I might come back another day.

I assume I must have nodded. I can't remember.

"I'm very handy," he said. "It's fun to do things by hand."

He bowed slightly.

"I'll miss you," I blurted out. "I may never see you again. I feel so alone."

"We are always alone: everybody by himself, like a shipwreck," he said. I grabbed his hands and held them in mine.

"See you soon," he said.

Fire-on-the-Water

• TARA L. MASIH •

I surprised my father tonight. The whole town of Monterosso, in fact.

We have lived by the Ligurian Sea for so long, we eat it, absorb it, breathe it. As children, we grew up with stories of how the sea saved us from Those Barbarians who were afraid of its power and would not venture down the sea cliffs. We were saved by the sea, over and over, in our history and in our bedtime stories.

But tonight, it turns on us. The incessant rains have pushed the water over the rivers' banks, flooding our seaside towns. And from the other side, the rough seas rage against the protective sea walls and the pebble beaches. The siren began an hour ago. I look out from behind the shutter to see our old fishermen trying to save their *lamparas*, stored on the coarse shingle for the usually mild winter.

My mother likes to say my father's eyes match the color of the sea because of generations spent fishing and swimming in them. When I was young, he used to take me out at night in his wooden spotlight boat. We'd row along the sea beds, the lamps torching out over the black water to find the fire-on-the-water, the green glow of luminescent plankton that draws in the "bread of the sea," the anchovies. But I did not want to be there. I did not have the patience to sit in that glow for hours, waiting for the sea to churn to a gray froth of fish, to haul them all in with the old, knotted, spiky nets. It was long, dull, painful work, and when we pulled into the beach to meet my mother, waiting with her terracotta pots to gather them, the haul seemed paltry and meager and not worth the time.

Most of us in town grew up with the smell of the smoke house sheds doing their work in the backyards, and with the smell of brine and fresh fish in the house as mothers gutted and scaled and stuffed the red, inner flesh. We helped them gather the scales' pearlessence so it could be trucked off and ground into lipstick and fake pearls and God knows what else. We watched them walk the *sentiri* trails along the sea cliffs to the neighboring villages to trade. And we knew we would not be making this same trek. We took our bikes and cars up the mountain and away, down the flat highways to the cities.

But now, I see a blue *lampara* disappear under a wave almost tidal in proportion, and when the wave drags back, the boat is gone. And I hear the dim cries go up from the crowd below. Muffled wails of such despair. The sea has turned on us in the past, but never like this, not with so much power and ability to take all.

I run out of the cliff house and down the slippery stone stairs to the main town road, cross the playground and fight my way against the rain and wind, pushing to get to the others. It is like a wall of resistance I have to break through. The siren continues to call out. When I reach the beach, I see my friend Carlo already there, and Vanni, the son of the cheesemaker. I join in the fight to save the colorful boats that our ancestors built and mended with such respect. As the sea tries to take one from me, I groan and bleed and fight to hold on, fall on my side. Looking up, I see my father crawling against heavy currents to reach me, and I catch a shimmery gray glint of something about to overflow from his eyes.

The Mystery Spot

• TARA L. MASIH •

Tea cups remain full these days. More for comfort than for quenching thirst, the Red Rose that cools within the patterned bone china. There is a small corner Christmas tree, it's the day after Christmas, 1941, and the peppermint-patterned packages are still wrapped. Tinsel silvers the limbs hung with a few tin ornaments she received as wedding gifts. The tree so full of wishes a week ago, now drops dry needles. She is so lonely, she hears them whisper against the paper as they fall.

War news on the radio interrupts this young woman's trance. Patriotic music brings her back. She glances to the heavy black phone that hangs by the stove, not ringing enough. The Navy, the Red Cross, days and nights go by since Pearl Harbor exploded. No word. His ship not accounted for. Could it have rained down into the vast ocean in pieces too small to collect? Could *he* have?

Her sister at the door the next day, not waiting for an answer, using her spare key, dressing her, driving her to the Mystery Spot. Things don't make sense in this spot, her sister explains while she exhales smoke from a thin cigarette. Vapors whorl around the closed car. The woman roles down her window to the cool California breeze. She wishes it were male hands on the steering wheel right now, not her sister's gloved ones.

They pay $1 for the new attraction, and the sisters watch balls roll uphill and brooms stand on end. They stumble in their pumps, feel light-headed near the pines whose branches reach in only one direction. They are told by the guide that the antigravity pull that swirls around the spot they are standing on is a vortex of magnetic fields. The woman wonders about the fact that there are still so many things in life that can't be explained.

Evening, just before the sun disappears, she draws the blackout curtains across the window panes. Talk on the radio is that it might be the end of the world. She hardly speaks these days. Some mysteries being too tragic for words.

• • •

The woman can't remember what day it is exactly, but she knows it's her birthday because her granddaughter shows up to take her to see MoMA's new rain room exhibit as a present. The woman wears a pin that is silver writing in a scroll: Remember – Harbor, with a real pearl in place of the word. It hangs heavy on her left breast. Over her arm, the Chanel umbrella her husband gave her 20 years ago. Because of her age and the intense heat, the crowd shuffles them to the beginning of the long waiting line. It is July 5, 2013.

When they are finally let into the room, the air is cool, water rains down, a spotlight highlights the cascade. This is something the woman wants to do on her own. She leaves her granddaughter's arm and shuffles across the grate. This new modern mystery. The rain parts for her. To others, she looks like an ancient dancer winding down as she turns, arms outstretched at bent angles. Being surrounded by falling water yet not getting wet, controlling the rainfall like a god, to her, it is a pure moment. Like the one when she heard his voice again, crackling through the ether, after a month of the unknown. Rain sluices down, pulses, intuits its own space around her, and her memories of joy slip through.

She reaches the end of the installation and a guard helps her off the metal floor. She nods as if she knows him, starts to tell him how she survived the end of the world. The woman's granddaughter and the guard exchange knowing smiles. She catches their look and bites down on her wayward tongue. They don't understand yet.

She leaves the rain room behind, ignoring the sign that tells visitors how it works.

Amps

• MICHAEL MCGILLOWAY •

My amp is a Peavey XXX. It's all tube. The cabinet is a Hartke; it's got a black grill. At some point someone was too loosey goosey at a show I was playing and he spilled something in the top. Smoke came out. I replaced the fuse, still wouldn't turn back on. I replaced the tubes and it worked for a few hours then shut off again. It's still in my garage.

My amp is a Twin Reverb. It's sitting in my basement right now with a huge mess of wires hanging out the back. My basement is like an amp graveyard. Sometimes it's fun just to plug in to the different amps that can still turn on just to see how fucked up they sound. I don't know how amps work at all.

I play through two amps actually, a Music Man and this weird one my friend rigged up. The problem is one of my cabs is busted. I've been messing with it for weeks in my bedroom but I don't think I'm gonna be able to salvage it. I also have no idea what I'm doing with electronics in general.

In my basement are the wrecks of like seven different amps. I think I'm gonna let a friend of mine use some of it for an art project. There are a lot of black grills, big black pieces of plastic, pieces of black metal and some gold painted stuff as well . . . lots of cool-looking busted electronics parts; shattered tubes, burnt-out tubes, stuff like that. I'm worried it might be dangerous though. I know enough about electronics to know that things like big capacitors can be really dangerous. Fun story about that: my friend Marc went to the hospital from trying to smash up an old TV to make it easier to throw out. Exactly what I'm talking about: there was some giant capacitor in it and he hit it with a hammer I think? Anyway he did something to this capacitor and it gave him this terrible nerve damage. Marc was fucked up for years with different opiates and stuff but he definitely didn't recover from the capacitor thing.

I got my Music Man when I was in high school. It was so awesome for so long but it started fucking up the other day. The problem is I don't know what I'm doing and I spend too much money on food and beer and stuff to fix it.

I was thinking about this one day: I don't really live in a musician house but I play in a band, so I keep my stuff in the basement and sometimes I play down there too. But the point is that's all I have down there: one amp, one guitar, some cables. I have friends whose houses are filled with broken amps and guitars and stuff. So what I was thinking is, what does that add up to in raw materials? How much plastic, metal, glass, wood, etc. went into making these big fat black things that make really loud sounds and was it worth it?

My Crate is gone now. It was this shitty solid-state Crate that I used when I was playing basically just power-chords in Ducks. It shit out a lot and I hated it and this dude trying to start a pop-punk bought it off me for like $100. So basically the only thing I have is the dumb busted Line 6 Spider in the basement.

Pan-America

• JEN MICHALSKI •

The couple at the four-mile marker of the trail has the smallest Yorkie you've ever seen. It eats from a collapsible bowl under the picnic table. The woman offers you a drinking glass as you curl your head under the outdoor faucet.

"Hard to get enough like that," she explains. You take the plastic tumbler and fill it. The people who frequent hiking trails are either super nice or super crazy. Sometimes they're both. You consider this as you join her at the table, where she is spreading egg salad on wheat bread. Her husband, muscular, head covered in a bandana, repacks their SUV.

"Cute." You reach under the table and the Yorkie jumps on your palm, licking it. Its enthusiasm would be annoying in a normal-sized dog, but you can hold her in your hand. "Is she still a puppy?"

"Princess is eight." The woman stops, admiring her work. "She's been to 48 states."

"Military?" The water is soothing down your throat. This much water, so early on in your 20-miler, is a luxury and a danger.

"He's a contractor." She nods toward her husband. "We're living in Aberdeen. They're a little weird out there."

"Generally, the farther out you venture out from the city . . . "

"You know what our neighbors did?" She holds up the clear plastic knife. You imagine her packing supplies this morning, the dog bowl, grapes. "They found a little poop in their yard and tied it to our front door in a baggie. And it wasn't even hers—it was probably a deer's or something. They think I'm Paris Hilton or something because I drive a Mercedes and have a little dog."

"That seems unreasonable." You agree. "Maybe you'll move again soon enough."

"I hope so." She tops the sandwiches. "But you never know which

America you're moving to."

You are not sure what to make of her, her serious running shoes, her Mercedes, her toy dog. Her husband has finished packing the Pan-America, which sounds more like an airline than an SUV, and sits at the table, not looking at you. The dog lies on her back in the grass, wriggling back and forth.

"We have to be careful." The woman looks at Princess. "Sometimes the hawks swoop down to grab her."

"She's precious. I'd be careful, too." You stand. "Thanks for the water."

"They found that girl not far from here," she says between mouthfuls of egg salad. Her husband coughs. "You read about her?"

You haven't, but you nod.

Later, they scare the shit out of you after you've run another two miles, on a shady part of the trail. They're on bikes, and she turns slightly and waves as she passes. Princess rides in a basket on the front of her bike, and her husband has a mini boom box strapped to his. It's hard to place the music—not country, not rock 'n' roll, but something soothing, like in a grocery store. He pedals past you, controlled, erect, like someone bringing forth a truth to this world.

Shale

• SUSAN SMITH NASH •

"Lost again!" said Durbin. "Google Maps and GPS are worthless out here in western Oklahoma. At least we have a signal. That's a miracle in and of itself."

Durbin and Marchande were on their way to oil and gas operations in the middle of a vast oil and gas play west of Oklahoma City which included the Woodford shale. They were checking on the microseismic monitoring stations to make sure that they had been installed correctly.

There had been complaints that the data looked strange.

Ideally, by monitoring the microseismic events created by the multi-stage hydraulic fracturing, they would be able to tell the oil and gas operator the height of the induced fractures, along with the pathways. The fracture networks were important because if they could be kept open using the proppants (100-mesh sand grains) they would be conduits for the flow of oil and gas, but only if they possessed sufficient connectivity.

"I wonder how many people know what it takes to produce oil from shale. A mile beneath our feet are 10 horizontal wells that extend out at least a mile and a half. Each one was drilled from the central pad," said Marchande.

"Yup. In a diagram, it looks like a 10-legged spider. The pad where the drill rig sits is the body," added Durbin.

"Shale. So misunderstood. Source rock, and now reservoir, too. It's the kitchen. It's where kerogen from ancient pond scum and algal slime gets turned into oil. Just add heat and pressure," said Marchande.

"I wonder why no one ever says shale is the womb?" asked Durbin.

"Good question," said Marchande. "My guess is that the whole concept is too dark, too cthonic. For me, it's all about Goethe."

"Like the Witches' Kitchen in Faust?" asked Durbin.

"Hah, yes! So. Welcome to Heidelberg, Oklahoma," said Marchande.

"What have you traded your soul for today? Knowledge? Riches? Fame? Expect your poodle, Yvette, to turn into Mephistopheles any time now."

Durbin laughed, but it was not convincing.

The wind had picked up. They had passed through mile after mile of wind turbines which Durbin claimed gave him a strange ringing in the ears.

"I read that Oklahoma is now #4 in the nation in the generation of electricity by means of wind energy," commented Marchande.

"Crazy," said Durbin. "So few people, so much energy."

"True," said Marchande. "And what good does it do them? They're smart. They're entrepreneurial and quick. And so—the first thing you know, there's an over supply and the price collapses."

Durbin nodded.

"Oh, yes," he said. "I remember the situation with natural gas. It was $12/mcf. Now it's around $2/mcf. The same with wind energy. And, now— oil prices. They've bottomed out."

The wind had picked up, and Marchande looked at an enormous American flag which rippled majestically against a backdrop of rolling hills covered with prairie grasses.

"That's the story of Oklahoma's economy. Boom-bust. It's easy to blame the victim, but we're collateral damage in this bust. We did not overproduce. In fact, the U.S. still imports 50 percent of its oil. No. Oklahoma is contributing to oil independence and energy independence, with wind energy. We're just the unmourned victims of a geopolitical game."

"I'd call it economic warfare," said Durbin.

"Yes, and the double-edged sword of technology. It works, but not well enough," said Marchande.

"Technology that doesn't work well enough? Double-edged sword? I hate to hear you say that," said Durbin.

"But it's true. Massive plays are massively expensive. Massively complicated. And, then, at the end of the day, it recovers 10 percent of the oil in place, and it declines within 24 months to the point of not producing anything except saltwater.

They stood for a moment and watched the prairie grasses bowing down in the breeze. In the distance was a cluster of cedar trees and a small pond. Marchande walked to the barbed wire fence and reached down to a leafy plant with prickly leaves.

"Check out the milkweed plant. They used to be everywhere. Now they're really rare. They say it's from using pesticides and genetically engineered crops."

Marchand leaned over and stroked the leaf lightly with her finger.

"I remember I once thought I found a Monarch Butterfly chrysalis on the plant. Milkweed is what they eat," she said.

Durbin nodded.

"And now they're endangered. I read that their numbers have dropped off dramatically," he said.

"One more example of collateral damage in a bigger conflict."

"It's an existential conflict, isn't it?" commented Durbin. "The existential anxiety of perceiving that you're always in a state of 'becoming' and never actually arriving, or 'being'—and that your travel to the state of beingness is fraught with risk."

"Always on the edge of extinction," added Marchande.

"The tragedy is that language itself is both the vector of both extinction and beingness."

"About which we cannot speak, we must consign to silence?" asked Marchande. "Wittgenstein lives on?"

"Hydraulic fracturing is all about intolerance of impermeability. We crave flow. Everything must flow. And, we try to control the way it flows, where it goes, and how long. What we do with what flows out—oil, gas, saltwater—we're not as worried about," said Durbin.

"And on the surface, we're all about the intolerance of diversity, although it's not what we claim to believe. If we really believed in diversity, why would we engineer so much uniformity—in plants, animals, even people."

A hawk circled slowly in the sky.

"Look. A hawk. Endangered, too. Pigeons and doves, however, thrive," commented Marchande.

As they looked at the hawk, a pickup truck with SandRidge Energy blazoned on the door pulled up.

"How are you doing? I'm Ray Wheeler. Can I help you? Car trouble?" asked the engineer, who wore jeans and a denim SandRidge Energy company shirt.

"GPS stopped working and I forgot to bring paper maps," explained

Marchande. She walked through short grass to shake hands with Roy. A quick buzz of a rattlesnake joined the sound of the wind.

"No problem. I can help you. Hey, did you know you almost stepped on a rattlesnake over there? It's gone now."

Marchande startled. "Oh my God! I hate snakes."

Durbin walked quickly to where the buzz had sounded. "There it is—it's moving away from us."

He walked up to Roy and extended his hand.

"Roy, we're on our way out to a well that SandRidge is operating. You may be just the person we needed to find."

Marchande was not paying attention. She was looking out toward where the rattlesnake had slithered away.

What a shame, she thought.

The reality of a rattlesnake and milkweed were supplanted by algorithms and images, patently not real. They were attempting to create mathematical models of the possible fractures induced by hydraulic fracturing, all taking place in the shale.

The shale represented the convergence of the real and the unreal, a place of pure impossibility. Like language, like self, like reality—all largely unknowable, but also the place of dreams.

Oil would flow, but only briefly. Life would seem infinite, and the creatures of the awkward, rough edges would face extinction.

And finally, all that is or was organic would become viscous and equally unknowable in the dark, deeply buried impossibility of shale.

The wind picked up again. The smell of sulphur was strong. Marchande's eyes watered as she turned from where the rattlesnake had hidden in the grass.

"I'm ready."

Playa de los Muertos
• SUSAN SMITH NASH •

La vida es tragedia, y la tragedia es perpetua lucha, sin victoria ni esperanza de ella; es contradicción.

—Miguel de Unamuno,
Del sentimiento trágico de la vida (1912)

There were just too many parallels and bizarre synchronicities, and so I just never could quite convince myself it was not a waking dream or a hallucination. Perhaps it was. It would be easier, in a sense, if it were. It was the second of November, the Día de los Muertos, and we made our way down a narrow, rutted road clogged with individuals carrying bright orange cempasúchitles (marigolds), the Aztec flower of the dead. Our destination was the Playa de los Muertos (Beach of the Dead), a beach at the edge of the cemetery, halfway down the coast in the state of Nayarit, the birthplace of the mystic poet (and ambassador) Amado Nervo. We passed through a small cemetery with pastel-colored above-ground crypts, with statues and figurines. We parked next to a robin's egg blue crypt and I pulled my towel around my waist, adjusted the light brown sandals I had purchased in Kaneohe Bay in a store near the entrance of the Marine Base. I remembered very clearly the day I purchased the sandals—it was a few months before a Chinook, a large troop transport helicopter was shot down. It was not my son's unit, but he knew many of the victims nonetheless. I wondered if my feet could feel vibrations residual from the day. And then I walked to the edge of the water. The sea was weirdly calm, and the salt water did not burn my eyes, and the sand below me stretched out below me in light honey colored waters that made me think of the cempasuchitles and the quiet faces of the relatives visiting the tombs of their loved ones. It was all too silent to conform to the stereotypes I held of Mexico and raucous, riotous, Dionysian rituals. But, perhaps that was yesterday. Today, all was muffled as I moved across the waters, the strangely becalmed state making me feel strong and confident. It was not at all what I would expect when all around me were echoes and reminders of not only mortality but also how transitory yet joyously beautiful are the moments in which we feel contact with something that makes us feel truly alive.

An Empty Lot Across the Street
• SUSAN SMITH NASH •

¡Eternidad! ¡eternidad! Éste es el anhelo: la sed de eternidad es lo que se llama amor entre los hombres; y quien a otro ama es que quiere eternizarse en él.

—Miguel de Unamuno,
Del sentimiento trágico de la vida (1912)

The feral cats were copulating in the lot across the street. This was something I had never seen before, and I found it utterly revolting. There was a large yellow cat crushing a small gray one. Across the yard, in a clump of gray-green grass, and hunkered down against the faded brown dirt, another cat—this one with a half-torn ear, waited his turn. In the meantime, in the yard next door, caged roosters crowed. Something made me want to record it: crowing, caterwauling, and shrieking in protest of the death crawl toward certain oblivion. How do you combat life/death cycles? The answer is that you can't. At least you can pretend it does not exist. Yesterday, I learned that the former manager of the Norris Conference Center in CityCentre in Houston had decided to quit and move with her recently retired husband to Los Cabos, Mexico. I have visited Los Cabos twice, and what I remember of it makes me think that it might as well have been on a different planet from here. In Los Cabos, I saw mile after mile of pristine condos, homeowner's associations taking care of manicured gravel and cactus yards, maintaining the painted walls and guard huts in muted earthtone color schemes. Here, a few hundred miles south on the Pacific coast, just northeast of Puerto Vallarta, all exploded in riots of overwrought, overheated tropical colors, all melting or peeling within days. In the same Norris Conference Center, I chatted with a young woman, probably around 30 years of age, taking the trash from the women's restroom. She was well groomed, with skin the color of light cafe au lait, dark hair neatly pulled back into a ponytail, and small gold earrings. She was originally from Nayarit, and I asked where. She said from the "sierras" and I visualized the gorgeous, tropical mountains that overlooked the coast where the cats and roosters were busy announcing their cycle of life, and I remember a Canadian retiree waiting in line in the airport describing all the great mountain biking east of Puerto Vallarta. The problem was that there was no work, she explained. Life was untenable. But, speaking of the reverse migration, what made life so untenable in Houston? Traffic? Cost? And, in my own world, what is it that pushes me, dogs me to migrate, if not physically, out of my own soul? And, who resonates with my own state of being? The young Mexican woman from Nayarit working at the Norris? The former manager of the center who had bought a condo in Los Cabos with her husband? Or, the roosters in cages, or the cat crushed into the dirt by the overwhelming desire of someone or something else?

Gray Matter

• LIZ TYNES NETTO •

"Oh, they warned me about you," Dr. Sars said, pulling down his surgical mask.

I had a job videotaping surgical procedures at a university hospital. Ostensibly, the footage would be used as a teaching tool, but the doctors, even those professing bravado, were suspicious at first. I mean, what if they made a mistake on camera? Plus, they couldn't blast The Black Keys on a boom box during a 6-hour triple bypass, crack jokes, and flirt with the nurses when a chick was in there taping the whole thing. I might as well have worn a sign that said, 'Fun-sucking, malpractice threat' taped across my borrowed scrubs.

The gig started in Orthopedics, with muscled guys drilling screws and plates into bone. I was with the Heart team after that: *aorta, left ventricle, defibrillation, palpitations,* the soft vowels and thrumming consonants would play in my ears long after I'd gone home, when I lay sleepless on my futon, wishing for the boyfriend I'd sent packing, listening to the beating in my chest. *Systolic, diastolic, the patient must be supine.* It's true that I had not loved him anymore, but still, I did not know why that was so exactly, and now it felt like a terrible failure on my part. One afternoon the chief cardiac resident placed a stethoscope, as cool as a gun, to my chest and listened. "You have an innocent murmur," he declared. But I knew better.

Soon, you get to know most of the surgeons by sight, no matter what their specialty. When Dr. Sars scrubbed in, he was shorter and a bit stouter than his colleagues. He looked more like a baker than a world-class brain surgeon. I'd asked the other doctors about him though. Hands like a safecracker, they said. A Kasporov of brain surgery, they said. Sick Ass Russian Surgeon. Dr. Sars

Finally, here he was, his arms out wide as if to welcome me, but it was only so a nurse could dress him in a paper gown.

"I'm sterile," I said from the doorway.

"A shame," said Sars with a wink.

"I mean——"

"No, of course." He gave a slight bow. "Come in."

I took a step into the room and looked behind him, at the head on the bed, shaved and painted with iodine. The head was getting scalped, basically. The residents were peeling back the man's skull, like you might a tough, fleshy fruit—a mango that revealed a coconut, a coconut with a mustache. A cop, I thought. A detective.

"May I?" I said, wanting to get closer. I was good at this little interim job. I was undeterred by gore, brokenness, the abject sadness a sick body can exude. I'd done all that when I buried my wreck of a father in grade school, nursed my parchment papered grandmother in high school, pulled out my own rotted tooth in a college dorm bathroom.

"Sure," said Sars, waving a sharp tool, and I came up beside him just as he began to saw into the skull. A camera can't capture the smell of a live human skull being sawed open. It can see how the piece pops out like a puzzle and is carefully saved in a little labeled plastic baggy. It can see the shiny gray mass beneath but not smell the savage, flinty odor of burnt fruit, a deep funk sharpened into a tang. Some people say it reminds them of the smell of Doritos.

"What do you think you're touching?" I asked, as the surgeon probed his tools deeper into the glistening brain, trying to find the bleed.

"The frontal cortex, this is on the left side so maybe I'm touching some language centers. We don't want to compromise language, so I need to be careful." The thought of that metal scalpel scraping against talking made me wince.

"Do you know who he is? Why he has a moustache?" I asked.

"Like, is he a cop? Or some member of The Village People?" asked Sars. We stood together over the brain.

"Or Stalin?" I said.

The patient's forehead was flapped over to the end of his nose but his moustache, mouth, and chin were clearly visible.

"Yes, Stalinische," he nodded.

After that, Sars continued digging and then he slowed. He gave orders, asked for new instruments, and gave more orders. He kept digging. The lamps overhead were hot and bright. The tiniest beads of perspiration formed at Sar's temple. I filmed close-ups of the tiny tools tunneling through nests of white neurons, like one day we might shoot through the Milky Way. I filmed wide. The team gathered around the exposed brain, the head nurse who handed the tools, the anesthesiologist monitoring the stats, the residents, everyone working in such concentrated harmony it felt like being inside a piece of music playing at a frequency inaudible to the human ear. I felt Sars' breath pushing through his mask at my neck when I leaned in tight. He kept on. Finally, it began to look like the bleed was close to staunched and closed.

"I wonder if his brain will remember this," I said, standing over the open head, as the team took a moment to breathe and shuffle about. "Any chance he'd remember the intrusion?"

"Let's see," said Sars. He pushed the lens of my camera away and pulled us down inches from the man's exposed, pulsing, ridged gray matter. "This is Bess and Dr. Anton Sars. We're in your brain," he whispered. "Will you remember us?" He turned to me and gave my shoulder a nudge.

I felt a sudden tenderness for the brain, so vulnerable and exposed.

"We love you," I said to the brain. It felt good to say something kind. It fed an ache. "We don't know you, but Dr. Sars fixed you and we love you."

"That was a stupid thing to say. Is that thing on?" Dr Sars said, pointing at the microphone, which was now on the floor with the camera.

"No," I said, lying.

"This guy killed a woman today," he said. "Shot a cop too." He shook his head and pulled down his mask. "He wrecked on his motorcycle, trying to escape." He gave the tired, wry smile of someone who'd seen a lot of all that.

But me, oh, I hadn't thought of saving bad guys, women killers, no less.

"Well, scrap it then," I said, leaning back over the brain, the murderer's brain, and lifted up my mask. "Fucking asshole." Like I was my mother, ten years ago, hissing over my passed out dad. Oh, this was fun. "Useless, fuck," I said with feeling.

The head nurse laughed. "I'll second that," she said leaning over the brain.

Then the anesthesiologist chimed in, with a merry, "Rot in hell, sick bastard."

A scrub tech said, "Die, die."

Sars stepped back and allowed the rest of the team to approach the open head. The three residents came forward, the remaining nurses—everyone filed past and whispered deep curses in the patient's exposed, gelatinous brain.

"Okay, wrap him up," said Dr. Sars with a whistle. He pulled off his apron and snapped off his gloves.

Months later, the trial was in the local news. By then I was filming other things—junkies in recovery, soldiers returning from Iraq. Moustache man went to prison for twenty-five to life.

Sometimes I think of him lying in his cell, and how he'll never know we slipped those curses into his frontal lobe before the patch was put on, before his head was wrapped up tight. He won't even know the weloveyou, as he pays for his crime, lying on a cot staring at the wall.

Of course, I checked the tape before handing it over to the hospital's audio-video department. You could only hear the hiss of the ventilator and the soft shuffling of slippered feet. There was no need to erase anything.

We were there and we said those things, but if you hear the tape, it's as if we never talked into that man's brain at all.

Fall

• DEBI ORTON •

My ghosts have always seemed to haunt me most in fall. I think it's because the line between the the living and the dying is clearer then. You can see things dying, you can count your losses by the day.

One day, the trees on the hill across the street have leaves. Two days later, those leaves are a riot of color, the trees standing shoulder to shoulder on the hill like a gaily dressed children's choir. Two weeks later, they are bare, dark and depressing.

Where I come from, old wives talk about fall being the time that most folks die. They say it's because of the changes—in temperature, in nature's rhythms. They say it's just a natural time for things to die.

"It must have been her time," they said, nodding sagely. They milled around at the funeral home, gossiped with each other and patted my hand. "So sorry, dear," they told me. Thousands and thousands of words from their mouths, and probably no more than a hundred of them different from one another.

I stood in the graveyard next to your casket on that cloudy, misty day like the host at a formal party, accepting murmured phrases meant to comfort me at a time like this. The people at the cemetery—not many of them, really—not knowing what to say, awkward about it and feeling a compulsion to say the same things they always say.

But they don't understand, don't know what it's like to have found the missing half of your self. They can't imagine what it felt like to have that once-missing half ripped away in one foolish instant. They tried to guess. But what you and I had is something totally outside their frame of reference.

That night, I made a pot of Earl Grey. Just the way you taught me, steeping it ten full minutes in the cozy. I poured a cup and went to our bedroom. Your clothes were still in the closet, and when I pulled them to my face, I smelled you. Why? We laundered our clothes with the same detergent, in the same washer, in the same load. How can your clothes smell like you while mine don't?

It broke my heart. I sat on the bed, placed my cup on the nightstand and wailed. The first time I broke down. I'd been afraid to, but there was nothing left to fear. The worst had happened.

"She'll come down when she's hungry," I told you, but you wouldn't listen. You took the ladder from the garage, leaned it against the tree. You made sure it was level, sturdy, solid. You climbed as high as you could and still couldn't reach that wayward kitten. So you leaned. And then you lunged for her.

The paramedics said it didn't hurt. It was instantaneous. You didn't suffer. I hold on to that like a handhold on a sheer cliff. At least you didn't suffer.

I went to bed in your pajamas that first night. But pajamas were your thing, not mine. Before morning, they were on the floor next to the bed, where they always landed when we made love. That memory brought a fresh needle of hurt, and I laid back, staring at the ceiling. My hands moved; I pretended they were your hands. They touched me here, like yours did, or there, like yours did. Nothing. I couldn't fool myself into thinking I'd have one last moment with you.

Suddenly, I couldn't lay in this bed; I couldn't be in this room, our room. I pulled on sweats and got into the car, driving aimlessly until I realized that it was light out, children were walking past me on the street next to the school where you taught. They were looking at me—a middle-aged woman dressed in an old chenille robe, stained T-shirt and sweat pants, blubbering like a kid whose birthday balloon has been popped.

It was still raining as I turned into the driveway. There it was. That huge maple, still covered with yellow leaves, the ground littered with them, incandescent. The tree trunk is dark with rain, and the leaves glow with a buttery golden light. Tears blur my vision, and when it clears, there you are, your ghost, at least.

We are raking the leaves, and you have just shoved me into one of the piles. The leaves are yellow; the leaves on this tree are always yellow. A yellow so bright it makes your eyes hurt. We are both laughing, and when I try to rise, you take great handfuls of bright yellow leaves and bury me in them. I can smell them, wet fall leaves. I can feel them brushing my face, lodging in my hair. I wish I had died at that moment, before the kitten, before your fall.

I go into the house and exchange my robe for one of your oversized windbreakers. I pull my hair back into a ponytail; take off my slippers and put on your clogs. At the department store, I walk straight toward the back of the store. I know what I want. I pick it out, pay for it, put it in the trunk of my car.

The sky is turning darker, deep gray clouds against lighter ones. It will probably rain all day. Everything is dark. The bare trees are wet, dark. The house, with the clapboards we stained a deep forest green that last summer, is dark. The lawn has turned a dark green, tinged with brown. The only bright thing I can see is that damned maple.

I park the car and take my purchase out of the trunk, ready to use. I walk toward the tree, click the switch and pull the cord. I should have cut it down last summer. You'd be here now if I had.

The Buccaneer

• DEBI ORTON •

In the center of the city three major streets converge, and in the middle of the triangle they form, there's a small park. It was originally dedicated to the veterans of the Spanish-American War, but over the past decade has fallen into shabbiness. Now, FALN graffiti adorns the Rough Rider statue and most of the grass has died from the constant foot traffic.

Trees line its sidewalk, and a couple of broken-down benches stand between the trees. The rest of the city is well kept, with sturdy benches for weary pedestrians plentiful and in good repair. But here, the benches are decrepit, just like the denizens of the park they line.

I work here, in the 24-hour convenience store across the street. I see them day in, day out, in every season and every kind of weather. They come in here for beer and cigarettes, once in a while for some food. They're almost always shitfaced.

That's what one of the old ladies from the library complains about, when she comes in to buy a paper to read on her bus ride home. "It's awful," she says, shaking her head. "They're always drunk! And the smell . . . " She doesn't finish the sentence. She doesn't have to. I'm so familiar with the smell of stale urine and sweat that I can conjure it up from just those three words: And the smell . . .

When it's slow, I watch them as if they're a cable channel—Drunk TV. These men aren't just homeless. They're hopeless, too far gone from years of hard living and cheap alcohol (or worse) to imagine that life could be lived any other way.

I know most of them by name, but one man only refers to himself in the third person: The Buccaneer. Something more than drink has addled his brain, and from the lengthy and spirited conversations he often holds with himself I think he may be schizophrenic.

I have no idea why he calls himself The Buccaneer, but it suits him. He strolls up and down Northern Boulevard like an officer inspecting his ship's deck. Passing pedestrians give him a wide berth, despite the fact that he usually grins back at them and touches the brim of his captain's cap deferentially.

At other times, he'll stand in the park, perfectly still, with his head cocked like a dog listening to one of those whistles humans can't hear, wearing a look of fierce concentration.

Today, though, there's something different about him. He's agitated and he's walking in circles, bumping into the trees, running into other drunks and shoving them out of the way. When Oscar, a regular, comes in for a pack of cigarettes, I ask him about it.

"Ol' Buccaneer's just havin' a bad day," he mumbles. "Happens sometimes. Seen 'im cut a guy for lookin' at him wrong. Long's you stay outta his way on days like this, you'll be fine." He pays me for his cigarettes and grabs them up, along with a fistful of the free matches. Once outside, he scuttles across the four-lane street, dodging the cars speeding up to beat the red light as he returns to the park.

When The Buccaneer approaches him, I see Oscar trying to back away. He holds his hands up in a universal gesture of placation, then reaches into his pocket and hands The Buccaneer a cigarette. Oscar makes his getaway while The Buccaneer is looking for his matches.

The park's almost deserted by noon, leaving The Buccaneer alone except for two guys stretched out on the benches. As oblivious as the rest of these guys are, they're not stupid. They seem to know that something bad's brewing, and they'd be safer somewhere else. The two on the benches are probably either too tired or too drunk to realize it.

When lunchtime comes around, the guys on the benches take off for the soup kitchen, leaving The Buccaneer there alone. Business in the store picks up for an hour or two, and it's nearly three before I get a chance to look outside again.

There's an ambulance with its lights flashing, a fire truck, and two police cars lining two sides of the triangular park. The fire station's only a block away, so I hear sirens all the time and have trained myself to ignore them. But it surprises me that I didn't realize one had stopped just outside. I yell to the owner that I'm taking my break and go outside for a smoke. The

113

regulars are all huddled together on the one side free of authorities, gawking as the paramedics tend to one of them lying on the ground.

The man on the ground is transferred onto a stretcher, and rolled into the ambulance. I see flashes of red and then the ambulance roars away. After a few minutes, the cops and the fire truck take off too.

Oscar has spent his day picking up cans further south along the Boulevard, and comes in around five with a bag full of empties, enough to pay for a couple of brews. I ask him what happened this afternoon.

"It was The Buccaneer," he says, popping open the beer and taking a long gulp before I've even given him his change. "He started givin' old Joe some shit, and Joe broke off a bottle and scooped his damn eye out with it." My stomach gives a little lurch, but Oscar's unfazed. "Tol' him he figured if he wanted to be a damned pirate, he should wear the eye patch." He wipes his mouth with the back of his hand and squints at the change I hand him. "Do I got enough here for some red hots?"

things her mother never told her
• LISA PRINCE •

rocks and potholes

things that are thrown and to be avoided. like words. sentences. the things in your head. you tiptoe past the obvious but the floorboards creak, always finding you out. revealing you in soft lighting. open windows and slamming doors. there is always a silent witness.

hot asphalt

burns feet and fingers. like a scab, you can't help but touch. peel back the surface. always peeking underneath to see what's hidden. disappointed when you reveal it's just more of the same. things scar over.

blinking traffic lights

there's always a warning sign. you chose to ignore it. proceed without caution. look surprised when you are broadsided and asked for insurance. certain it is not your fault. you pull out your papers only to find them out of date. premiums unpaid.

do not merge signs

things that should be heeded. like recipes and instruction manuals. always at the back of the drawers and cupboards. pulled out only for weddings and funerals. nobody can read the writing in the margins. you add your name to the scrawl.

the center line

things that should not be crossed over. you head into oncoming traffic without seeing it. cross roads without looking both ways. you stumble over curbs and sidewalk cracks. remember children's rhymes and wonder. was it always this way.

passing lane only

the place where you find yourself. alone and in the dark. crying into pillows. something is lost and something broken. sometimes they can't be distinguished. you've forgotten your name as you last saw it. signed it on a paper and walked away.

things I have forgotten
• LISA PRINCE •

mud between my toes

riverbanks are soft and giving. like your flesh beneath my fingers. a scent of fecundity. how life creeps in at the edges and washes you away. like so many summer storms—a flash of light and a sizzle of rain

rocks skipping out over water

in my hand you are clear, but when I look through you, you are depths that are hidden. like dreams and nightmares. things that crawl out only at night, slip between your covers and make silent bedfellows

a child's laughter

people are always milling about, crowding in places that they aren't welcome. like leaves in autumn falling from trees—only not as beautiful. colors muted. stringent voices always calling out to strangers

the smell of grass newly mown

color is pervasive. white in winter. red in summer. in-between times we pray for rain. consider puddles, tire tracks and railway ties. the garden is in full bloom but nobody notices, always looking at the sky

fireflies at dusk

you turn out the lights one by one, claiming to save money, but really in the dark you sit alone with your thoughts and pretend that no one else exists. I have seen you with your coffee mug, always drinking someone else's grinds

the color of your skin under moonlight

things are always more profound under moonlight. starlight. the cover of darkness.

you lie in bed, awake, feeling the empty space beside you and wonder if this weren't already tomorrow, where would she be?

things found in rain puddles
• LISA PRINCE •

a cell phone

all sources say a ziploc bag of rice will dry the circuits. I say sometimes there isn't anything to recover. you press buttons but no signal gets through. these are the three numbers you know by heart. by monday they will be forgotten

a rain boot

somewhere a child wanders with a muddy sock. his mother will scold and deny him supper. what no one understands is it was necessary. a certain equilibrium met by the presence of one yellow rain boot sitting in the water, mocking ducks

someone's sock

you would think this matches the rain boot, but the sizing is all wrong. a left foot instead of a right. the hunchback always struggling for the exit. bells ringing in the distance. you wonder at the clarion call. I count intervals instead

a pocketknife

the blade has rusted, and one mother of pearl siding has fallen off. though you run your fingers through the water, you won't find it. it's gone the way of diminished things. the broken. the lost. there are no explanations, but you ask anyway

two sticks and a rock

you are reminded of devil sticks. juggling. the clowns at the circus. in the distance a dog is barking. reminded of dinner. a walk. things left behind. the bark is broken with tooth marks, like scrapes down your back. things she has left you

a gum wrapper

silver and folded neatly into an origami crane. it bobs at the edges in time with passing cars. someone has written on the inside but until you smooth it out, all is hidden. your fingers smudge the ink, leaving you imprints. an X. a Y. two dots and a dash

your car keys

the reason for delving. mired in mud. your fingers come away gritty, dripping. sending ripples in the water. deliberate you stir things. like arguments. harsh words. epitaphs. things to be written on gravestones. all things end

my reflection

by the time you see me, I've already gone. migrated for winter. followed the air currents to more moderate climes. the echoes you hear are not me crying. just new fallen raindrops hitting pavement. their sound a staccato beat. the way you loved me

Revolutions Per Minute
• CHARLES RAMMELKAMP •

True, the sound from the GE Wildcat Portable Record Player was a bit muddy. Solid state stereo three-speed (33, 45, 78, though none of us ever had a 78 rpm record, which we associated with square old-time music, pre-rock-and-roll; we only used 45 for the singles and 33 for the long-players), quality equipment captured in that phrase that was just beginning to be used, "state of the art." (Note: Actually, the phrase "state of the art" was first coined in 1910, but its popular use in advertising dates to around 1967.) These days, of course you just click YouTube or MP3 or pop in a CD.

But I'm not here to talk technology. I'm here to talk about the lyrics in popular songs and the controversies they created among me and my friends, high school kids who routinely smoked cigarettes and listened to music after school. Those were the days you went down to the record store or the dime store and bought the latest Beatles or Stones record for $2.99/mono, $3.99/stereo, and cigarettes were thirty cents for a pack of twenty.

"He's singing the word 'pussy,'" Ross Burgess asserted.

"No he isn't!" three of us declared. You couldn't get away with a word like that in a popular tong, could you? True, we'd all tittered listening to Muddy Waters' "Got My Mojo Workin'." But nobody'd ever really defined what a mojo was the way they'd defined a pussy, right? Maybe a mojo wasn't a dick.

"Here, listen." Ross dropped the needle in the smooth space between the second and third tracks on side two. As if we held our breaths in anticipation, listening to the pops and static, we began to breath again when the acoustic guitar came on. Then the song:

I can't understand, she let go of my hand, and left me here facing the wall...

"You can't say 'pussy' on a record," Teddy Morris said with finality. "You just couldn't get away with it."

"Maybe the record company wasn't listening closely," Don Erdman speculated. "Can I have a Marlboro?"

Ross shook a couple of cigarettes out of his pack, gave one to Don.

"Well, it's Dylan." That said it all as far as Ross was concerned.

"Not even Dylan."

"Shh! Quiet!"

We all listened, rapt.

If I didn't have to guess, I'd gladly confess to anything I might have tried

"OK, it's coming here," Ross announced, and we all tried to listen closely to the song coming out of the portable record player, watching it spin around, one complete revolution approximately every two seconds, looking to the long tone arm that held the stylus, the needle resting against the record itself, as if it alone could unravel the mystery.

But now something has changed, for she ain't the same, she just acts like we never have met . . .

"There!" Ross declared. "Pussy ain't the same."

"He didn't say 'pussy'!" Teddy shouted, just as emphatic as Ross.

"Well then what does he say?"

"Can we play it again?"

We all groaned. The lyric was at least two minutes into the song.

"Let's ask Roger. He knows all of Dylan's lyrics," Don suggested.

"Roger's not here," I needlessly pointed out, though my intent was to say that we couldn't resolve the issue here and now. But I was thinking of the sadness of the song itself, how the guy is baffled by the way the girl just snubs him without explanation, after their previous intimacy. Couldn't she explain? She just acts like we never have met.

But Don's suggestion seemed to satisfy everybody else. Roger McCoy was our expert on Dylan; whatever he said would be right. Still, Teddy couldn't help but point out to Ross that he'd misheard the lyrics of "Satisfaction" as "fling cigarettes at me," when in truth Jagger had been singing, "the same cigarettes as me." It was a minor point, but Ross conceded it.

A Wise Man Said Nothing
• CHARLES RAMMELKAMP •

I never say anything during the Saturday synagogue discussion, after the Torah reading, which is not to say I don't find it interesting. Usually it's about stuff I just don't think about that much, though, don't really have an opinion about, like how to deal with Shemot—paper on which God's name is written; when is it permissible to recycle a piece of paper with God's name and when should it be placed in the geniza box to be buried. (I'd never even *heard* of a "geniza box" before we had this discussion. It's a temporary storage area in the synagogue where you put worn-out Hebrew-language books and papers prior to ceremonial burial. Who knew? I hadn't even been particularly aware of the seven divine Hebrew names for God and the way to finesse their spelling so as not to actually write them out. And I learned another new word, "tetragrammaton." Look it up sometime.)

Apparently since the advent of the printing press and the explosion of printed matter it's become a legalistic hot topic among certain rabbis. And don't even get them started on photocopiers and laserjet printers!

But on this particular Saturday I thought I might raise my hand, wait to be called on like a kid in class, offer an opinion. We were talking about assisted suicide and a young woman with terminal brain cancer who'd moved to Oregon because of its death with dignity law. It was October and we were early in the Torah cycle, and the direct biblical reference to hang the discussion on was the story of Noah in the early chapters of *Genesis*, where after the Flood, God allows Noah to kill animals for food, but with the proviso, "You must not eat meat that has the lifeblood still in it," which is all about the sacredness of life, and add to that the sixth commandment, *Thou shalt not kill*, which comes in the next book, *Exodus*, and you see where God was coming from on the issue.

Let me just say that there are certain people in the congregation who you can always count on to express an opinion. So there's never any pressure to express a viewpoint, make an observation, if you don't really want to. It's not like we're being graded on class participation. In fact, Gabe Kellerman, a lawyer (it figures) almost always starts off the discussion, and he did this day, going on about proposed death with dignity legislation in Pennsylvania that allows terminally ill adults to obtain dosages of lethal medications from their doctors to self-administer, the way it's done in Oregon, more or less. Certain Catholic bishops were up in arms about it, of course, very vocal about their opposition

The question here was what the Jewish perspective is. Of course no Jewish official was ever going to condone suicide, but then again, when you got into the gray area of "quality of life" and "suffering," things got a little dicey.

After Gabe got it going, the rabbi was recognizing people right and left who wanted to say something, usually in support of assisted suicide, it seemed to me.

"The Talmud observes that no rites are to be observed for somebody who takes his or her own life with the full knowledge of his or her actions," Mark Rosenbloom put in sagely, when it was his turn. Mark's some sort of surgeon. We used to talk basketball scores when our kids went to the same Jewish day school years ago and we were picking them up at the same time. Now our children have grown up and have lives of their own and I probably haven't said a word to Mark beyond a polite, "Good Shabbos."

"The Hebrew word is *b'daat*, by the way, when you take your life with the full knowledge of what you're about to do," Mark continued. "So—no eulogies, no rending of clothes. Whatever rites are done out of respect for the dead, you aren't supposed to do them.

"But there's another category of suicide that encompasses those who are under severe mental strain or physical pain—like the young lady in Oregon. Jewish law calls this type of suicide an *anuss*, a 'person under compulsion.' King Saul was the first *anuss*, impaling himself on a sword in First Samuel after the Philistines defeated the Hebrews on Mount Gilboa."

Mark knows his shit, and this seemed to cover everything as far as I could see. No doubt the discussion was coming to an end now, and we'd move on to the *musaf* prayers before breaking for lunch. What else was there to say?

But the whole thing made me remember my mother in her last years, how after breaking her hip and being consigned to a nursing home for several months, in a semi-private room in a ward full of the drooling, doped and depressed—most of them just waiting there to die, as if in some sort of limbo, people she'd once known and spoken to if she'd met them in public, but had just lost track of once they'd come *here*—she'd resolved to lay in a supply of whatever it was she'd need to take her life, if she ever got to that state of helplessness again and was about to be carted off to the nursing home.

I don't know if she ever did. God knows she had a full array of pill bottles already for the various ailments that came with her age, but if there was poison, I never found it. Not that I was looking for it.

But the mission of the last year and a half of my mother's life was to avoid the nursing home, to die in the peace of her own home, where she'd lived for nearly sixty years, the house where my brother and I had grown up, the house she'd shared for so many years with my father, the house in which he himself had died twenty years earlier, the result of a massive heart attack.

My mother was at home when the end came. One morning her caretaker came over and found my mom in distress. Her heart and her kidneys, it turned out, were both failing, and the medication for the one only exacerbated the other; I never fully understood, but that was the substance. She was checking out, no way to save her, and she didn't *want* to be saved. She told the caretaker to just let her die, but Charlene called an ambulance, and she was taken to the hospital, and that's when the palliative care doctor called me and my older brother, both of us living lives hundreds of miles away from Potawatomi Rapids.

My brother Leon's an actor in Los Angeles, not a very successful one but he ekes out a living and he's doing what he loves to do. I remember how proud my parents were when he had the lead in *Hamlet* in our little Michigan high school senior class play. It's what launched his career, his life, really, and all the choices he would subsequently make.

How our parents swooned at the end, especially our mom, when Leon, dressed in his royal Renaissance duds, staggered, clutched his guts, bent over from the poison, put the back of his hand to his forehead and declared to Bobby Foster in the role of Horatio, "I cannot live to hear the news from England. But I do prophesy the election lights on Fortinbras. He has my dying voice. So tell him, with the occurrents, more or less, which I have solicited. The rest is silence."

I couldn't tell if my father was really that impressed, but mom was literally weeping.

Anyway, after I got the call from the palliative care nurse, I flew in from Baltimore, went to the hospital, arranged with them to bring her home for hospice care. It's where she wanted to be, in the hospital bed we set up in the dining room, looking out the back through the big picture window, though what she could see, what she was conscious of, I couldn't have said.

Over the next few days, friends came, held her hand, stroked her face.

Occasionally she would wake as from a nightmare and croak to me or Leon, as we sat vigil, "I want to die! Please kill me! I just want to die!"

During one of her wakeful moments, as she fixed me with that ancient mariner's look of plea which only made me feel all the more helpless, I held her hand and told her, "You were a great mother," feeling a bit like an actor myself, speaking the lines I could only say once and for which I hadn't been prepared, and suddenly very self-conscious about using the past tense and wondering how much she comprehended of what I was saying, or if she was hearing me at all, whether that stricken look was for me at all or whether she was just swept up in her own pre- or post-verbal pain. I could never, never know. All that remained was silence.

Becoming gradually aware of a stirring in the congregation, I shook myself from my reverie and turned my attention to the rabbi at the bima, who was drawing the conversation to a close.

"We can continue this discussion during Kiddush luncheon," he was saying, "but now it's time to move on. Please rise for *hatzi kaddish*."

With a slight *ping!* of regret, I realized I'd missed my chance to say something, but it didn't last very long. What was there even to say?

Electroencephalography
• DON RIGGS •

It was a night. The cracked spider veins of lightning jagged across the surface of the cornea, reflecting the sparking of synapse leaps in the ganglia within. Hair stood on end, as if he had just inserted a fork into a toaster, trying to free the blackened bastard of cracked wheat.

The floor shifted uneasily, as if in an intermediate stage before the surge to the nearly vertical that would dash everything in the kitchen, especially the half-wakened man staggering across the deck, against the wall, now briefly horizontal.

The moon was a dim smudge in the slathered cloud cover. The crumbling pavement rose up to meet his soles and alternately fell away from them. Hands in pockets—what else could he do with them, wave at the weather?—he turned to notice one maple groping the gables of a Victorian mansion where the windows occasionally flickered with a bluish light. The maple seethed in what the man, projecting his usual pathetic fallacies over the out-of-doors, saw as sexual frustration. The house, indifferent, remained focused on its occasional inner eruptions.

Red light stabbed the night repeatedly, repetitively, repetitiously. The police car whined to a stop and the officer it had swallowed goggled out, a catfish struggling for breath from a stagnant pond, and said, "Hey buddy, you all right?"

"Yeah, officer. Just taking my dog for a walk. Have you seen him?"

"Yeah, I think it was last year, over at the reservoir. You going there?"

"Only if I have to, officer. Only if I have to."

"I hear ya. Good luck, and watch out for the wombats."

"Night, officer."

"Night."

The patrol car growled off into a neighborhood where the acacia bushes were migrating across the lawns and gnawing on the garages. The pedestrian slogged on, slipping through the interstices between molecules.

He reflected—the random light flashed and glowed off his granular sparkling surface—that he had originally contacted the pet over the internet, where he didn't know it was a dog. Who knew what order of being was caught by that skein of diagonally intersecting lines, thrown out by a spider filament, filament, after filament until it finally connected and some other soul, or shoal, for those whose nets had a more ambitious catch in mind?

The stratus cloud layer covering the neighborhood—or, depending on one's perspective, covering the sky—had a heavy, layered look to it, impenetrable as a shelf of shale sliding between the various levels of being like a lightweight helium-filled Leviathan that was drifting through this corner of the cosmos. The occasional drops of rain began tasting a little of oil—shale oil, fracturing the conflicting mythoi of the atmosphere.

The Yomiuri Giants Win 3-0
• JOHN WOLFGANG ROBERTS •

It was a humid July morning edition, dated 1974. Baseball politics was all he read. Sanshiro sat at the breakfast table in his pajamas and slippers and turned to the Giants over coffee. At ninety-one, he'd been brewing his own for the last twenty-three years; wedding pictures still hung on the wall from the turn of the century. This was the house he and his wife built when he returned from the Liaodong Peninsula in Manchuria with shrapnel in his leg and partly deaf in the right ear.

The loose plank sidings over the years fell off the house revealing dried mud between the walls. Every year the roof put a heavier tilt to the structure and as time passed, Tokyo grew taller and the house slouched deeper in permanent shadow. And when construction officials came to speak to him about the location of his house, he never answered. They bowed to the silent door and walked away.

The property was now worth fortunes, nestled between train lines, toll roads, and scrapers that outdid each other every decade or so. Tycoons came to visit him, but they too were met with silence. "He's a stubborn old Dog," one Tycoon said loud enough to be heard through the door, sometime in the early 1990's. He walked off the property with heavy feet. This repeated for the next twenty some-odd years, that is, the same gray suits sporting different faces.

One day a Tokyo bureaucrat noticed a slight oversight: the property taxes had not been paid since 1974 and this 'ninety-one year old man' owed forty years worth of back taxes. The construction crew arrived at the old man's house, led by the thick-glassed and beady-eyed bureaucrat, who rarely had an occasion to leave the office. He ordered them to break the lock. When they entered, the bald Sanshiro sat with his back to the door, silver hair littered around the chair like waves around islands of tarnished steel.

Sanshiro's bony knuckles clenched the brittle news of the Giants beating the Dragons, while his pale gaze fixed upon the pictures across the room—as if returning to his wife from war, while drinking a cup of rainwater.

Bad Matches

• THADDEUS RUTKOWSKI •

When I came home, I found my live-in girlfriend lounging with a couple of her friends from the building. Two of them were sitting on chairs, and my girlfriend was lying on the couch. Her bare feet were propped on an upholstered arm.

When I asked what they were doing, they said they were tripping. "We each took a hit," one said.

"Of what?" I asked.

"Ecstasy," said another. "We were going to give you one, but there are none left."

"You're in an altered state all the time anyway," my girlfriend said.

I sat there and watched them smoke cigarettes. They had incredible stamina for staying in one place. I tried putting on music, but they told me to turn it off.

"You really are insensitive," said one.

They turned on the television to the *Donahue* show.

I baby-sat them for a couple of hours. When the drug wore off, the ones who didn't live with me went home.

• • •

Later, my girlfriend spent the night with a man she'd met through one of the women from our building.

"What's his name?" I asked.

"Scott."

"Scott?"

"Well, his real name is Maynard, but Maynard sounds like 'mallard.' A mallard is a duck, and a duck lives in the water. *The Great Gatsby* takes place on the water, and that book was written by F. Scott Fitzgerald. So I call him Scott."

"Did you actually sleep with him?"

"Of course."

"What the heck!"

"Don't worry," she said. "I'm moving out soon. I'm getting my own place with half of your money."

• • •

I called a woman I'd met at work. I hadn't seen her in years, but even so, she seemed happy to hear from me. She invited me to her place. I went to the edge of Manhattan, then walked into an apartment complex built on a landfill. She lived on a high floor of a tower.

Inside, every line was straight, every surface smooth. The lines where the walls met the floor were sharp and clean. There were no nail holes anywhere. I felt my compulsion meter rise. I wanted to mess things up.

"My sister is away," she said.

"I didn't know you had a sister," I said.

"She's a real estate agent. Nice place, huh?"

She turned on a stereo. I sat on the edge of a couch next to a low glass table. "Listen to the lyrics," she said.

I concentrated on the words and heard something like "I'm not your Weed Whacker, I'm just a strong black man."

"You know," she said, "I used to work as an exotic dancer."

"Where?" I asked.

"A truck stop on Long Island. The kind of place where you can get anything you want."

She tore a match from a book. "Here's a trick I learned," she said.

She split the cardboard stick partway, unbuttoned her shirt and placed the two pieces of cardboard around a nipple. The match stuck like tweezers. She took another match and lit it, then used it to light the unlit tip. We both watched as the match head flared.

The smell of burnt sulfur and the sound of rap music filled the air.

"What if your sister comes home?" I asked.

"I'll invite her to join us for tea and match tricks."

• • •

When I opened my apartment door, I could hear small paws running toward me. The cat that my girlfriend hadn't taken wanted food, so I opened a can and spooned out some of the mush.

I smoked a fake cigarette. The object looked like a real cigarette, with a white-paper barrel and a tan filter, but it was made of plastic. I took a few empty tokes to steady my breathing. I thought it would make me calmer, but it didn't. I needed something else. I picked up a racket and a tennis ball and slapped the ball around the apartment. I kept going for minutes without missing.

I still wasn't satisfied, so I chewed a stick of gum. I chewed for a long while, until the gum disintegrated in my mouth. The wad became granular, no longer taffy-like. I had to spit it out.

At night, the cat came and slept on my bed. Its nearness was a comfort.

• • •

My former girlfriend invited me for dinner. She was staying with a friend of hers, a woman she'd met at one of her brief jobs.

When I came into the kitchen, I could see that she'd used many utensils to prepare our meal. Pots and pans were everywhere. She'd always been good at cooking, but the cleanup (my job) had always been a big operation.

"Thanks for the food," I said. "It's very good."

"I followed what that person said on *Donahue*—you know, the cooking expert."

After dinner, we had sex the way we used to, except there were no props in the apartment. I had to borrow some of her silk scarves, and they worked fine.

She told me she loved me, and I said the same to her. But she didn't ask me to visit again, and I didn't invite her to return to my place, either.

• • •

Later, one of the women who lived in my building knocked on my door. I knew she wasn't looking for my girlfriend, because she knew she'd moved out.

"I left some Ecstasy here," she said. "It's in your freezer."

Sure enough, there was a frosty plastic bag in the ice compartment. I took it out and handed it to her. The bag contained one big pill.

"I'm giving it to Scott," she said.

She looked at me as if to say, "I hope you've learned your lesson, now that you have no girlfriend," but she didn't say anything as she left.

Between Places

• THADDEUS RUTKOWSKI •

I'm living in a rented house with my wife and daughter. We're sharing it with people we don't know. We have our own apartment, but sometimes we go into other people's rooms, and sometimes they come into ours. No one seems to mind this arrangement. We're leaving the house soon, anyway.

• • •

There is material on my work-computer screen that I don't want other people to see. I look at a window on the monitor, careful that no one is watching me.

Someone comes to my desk to ask a question, then sits at my keyboard and starts to type. The private content is one layer below what shows on the screen. The person won't leave my desk.

But maybe I'm wrong. Maybe the secret material is on my home computer, not my office computer. I wouldn't put those kinds of images on my computer at work.

• • •

I'm copying Chinese text onto sticks. I'm holding half a dozen pieces of wood that look like tongue depressors. The Chinese characters are aligned in vertical rows.

I'm finding these words in a source book, and they are being duplicated automatically on the wooden sticks, as if by a Xerox machine. I don't have to do the copying by hand. All I have to do is make my wishes known.

I'll show these coded sticks to people and hope they understand the words.

• • •

My wife, daughter and I are moving out of our apartment. We have only a few boxes and bags to pack, but I can't gather all of them. Each time I reach for something, I find something else I need to bring. I pick up a plastic bag, and I'm going to stuff it into a larger bag, but the larger bag is filled with cookies for our trip. I eat a couple of the cookies and leave the plastic bag alone.

The rooms now have no furniture, just carpeting and bare walls. I don't know what we slept on or sat on during our stay here.

• • •

My office has been moved to a new space, a sort of large terrace, with a slate floor. There is no office equipment, no desks or computers. There are some tables with wrought-iron legs—patio furniture.

The people I'm working with are new, too. They are taking over the operation. One is a woman—I used to work for a female boss. The new people seem nice enough, but I suspect they won't need me around much longer.

• • •

I decipher the Chinese characters I've copied onto sticks. The ideograms form a poem about drinking. The poet is spending the night outdoors and alone. After a few drinks, the moon and his shadow are his friends. The three of them do some singing and dancing. I understand his state of mind.

• • •

I go back to the apartment we've moved out of to see if we've left anything behind. I find a number of things, mostly shoes. There are about three pairs of my wife's shoes on the floor, and one of her shoes that has no counterpart. I look into a closet and see a couple of pieces of luggage: a large backpack and a long, thin case for something like a fishing rod or a rifle.

I see that I can fit these things into my backpack. Somehow, the larger pieces are collapsible. I'm going to have to carry all of this stuff with me to work, then bring it home when the day is done. My wife will be surprised and happy to see the retrieved items.

• • •

Our new apartment's front door is flimsy. It's a folding door with a small knob in the middle, at the seam. It looks easy to break into.

I've forgotten where the subway entrance is. It is far from our apartment, but it used to be clear in my mind. Now, I can't find it at all. I walk along unfamiliar streets, looking for the entrance.

When I get home, I see that my Chinese texts have been defaced. Someone has written sarcastic comments next to the characters and made serious words into jokes. "Moon," a scrawled note reads. "Ha!"

Otherwise, I see no evidence of breaking and entering. Nothing has been taken.

• • •

I come out to the car I've rented and see a traffic officer leaving a parking ticket on the windshield. "I'm going to move the car now," I say, hoping to avoid a fine.

It turns out not to be a ticket, but a crime report. "Someone broke into your car," the cop says.

I was carrying paintings in the car. The canvases were small, but some were valuable. I don't know where I got these paintings.

I also don't know if I'm able to drive. I broke my right arm months ago, but it's still weak. I can't lift it into a horizontal position without using my other, healthy arm. Once I get my hand on the steering wheel, I can clench my fingers and hold on for a while before the injured arm starts to ache again.

I look into the back of the car and see some jackets and hats—they haven't been stolen. Only the paintings are gone.

I'm waiting for my daughter. Obviously, I left the car parked too long. My daughter and I were inside a house, doing something, not paying attention to the car. Now, a lot has gone wrong.

• • •

Our daughter is going to China by herself. She is packing bags—she has several of them. They are not all suitcases. Some are shopping bags.

She has tasks here, where she lives. One is a big test in school. But she'll miss these duties while she's in China.

If she needs our help there, we won't be able to go. I don't even know how we'll communicate with her. She has Chinese hosts, but I don't know them. I'm not sure if they are trustworthy.

I always knew there would come a time when she would move away from home. I just didn't know it would happen this way.

"Don't worry," she says to me. "I'm not leaving yet. We have time to play a game. You know, the one where you and Mom hold my hands and swing me up while we're walking."

"I'll try," I say, even though I can't lift much weight with my injured arm.

The Stacker

• SCOTT STEIN •

The stack was developing as a sort of snowflake, with a symmetry as unconventional as it was unconditional. The columns at the snowflake's outer tips consisted of the rectangular crates, which grew larger as they neared the ceiling, and the crates with still more sides also grew progressively larger throughout the stack. The stack was sorted by code in a diagonal pattern, both alphabetically and numerically, and a chessboard arrangement had also emerged, with the alternation of light and dark wood crates throughout.

Had the Stacker intended all of it? Any of it? He didn't understand how it had worked out to such perfection. The pieces had just fallen into place. He couldn't believe the beauty he had brought into the world, and stood for a moment, still and silent and wondering how it had all happened. Finally, he had a stack that he wanted people to see, that people were capable of seeing. The other stackers would never tell him they liked it, he knew that. They would resent his accomplishment; their blind jealousy wouldn't allow them to acknowledge the greatness of his art. He didn't need them anyway. A stack as important as this one could not be long ignored.

With a synthesized chime and a flashing red light, the freight elevator's doors parted. For a full minute, the automated treadmill churned loudly as it steadily spewed more crates into the room. The Stacker laughed for a second. This was clearly a joke. There was never more than one delivery per day. Someone was having fun at his expense. Who could be playing games like this? No one. It was no joke. He had no friends, no one who would trouble with such childishness. And tampering with crates was a serious offense. No, this was a real shipment, and he would have to assimilate it into the rest of the stack. How could they do this to him? He looked at the perfection of the stack he had constructed, marveled at its purity, and was afraid to disturb it, to introduce new crates that might upset the harmony it embodied.

But looking upon it made him know that he had nothing to fear. He was now one of the Masters. The finest stack in history stood before him, fashioned by his own hands, and this new challenge could only result in further greatness. He strapped a crate and maneuvered it into position, and another, and another. The stack reached nearly to the ceiling. He worked even more frantically than he had the first time, and the stack grew in size and beauty. The symmetry continued, and the top half of the stack mirrored the lower, with the new crates now getting smaller as they approached more glorious heights. Certainly it would be the subject of numerous papers and articles. Probably the University would offer research grants to study it at length. The Stacker was sure to be made a supervisor. He would likely tour the country, speak to panels, and help with important decisions and policies.

He swung and hooked and strapped until his hands burned and his back ached. He ran and leapt and nearly danced as he became one with the stack, until he understood each crate as if he had built it himself, until his clothes were wet and his arms were heavy. Then, still sweating and panting, he realized that it was done. The stack was complete. Its giant shadow drowned out the light, and he stood, shivering in awe. He wished it weren't so dark. He couldn't get a good look at the stack, and turned toward the wall to brighten the light, but bumped into a crate instead. He was inside the stack, in the center of the immense snowflake, which was everywhere flush with the ceiling. The Stacker had walled himself in. He couldn't get out and couldn't see the stack from the outside, as it was meant to be seen. He had to find a way out. The collators would be by soon, there would be transfer requests, and he couldn't be found in this ridiculous position, trapped by his own creation. The greatness of his stack would be lost if it got out that he had imprisoned himself. The first thing one learned as a stacker was to leave a way out. The fundamentals had eluded him.

Just then there was a knocking from the hall. He didn't answer. A banging. He held his breath and was motionless. More banging, and the Stacker heard a sheet of paper being slipped under the door and then withdrawing footfalls. He was saved. He had bolted the door, and no one would be able to enter until he unlocked it himself.

The Stacker grabbed a crate and slowly began shimmying it loose. He had designed the stack so that he could remove crates when called upon without disturbing the integrity of the overall structure. True, he had intended to remove them only from the outside (after he'd shown the stack to the proper persons and had it photographed), but that shouldn't make any difference. He slid the crate from side to side before finally pulling it through.

There was a distant creak and a rumble, and the giant shadow wavered. The columns swayed slightly, and the Stacker ran to one and tried to hold it in place. There was a perfectly square hole where he'd pulled the crate loose, large enough for him to escape from the deteriorating stack, but he made no move toward it. He ran from one column to another, but the rumble grew louder and the wavering more severe. As the crates toppled from their height, he made no effort to evade them but struggled to brace the stack, still pitifully leaning into a trembling column when the first crate came down on his head.

The entire stack followed. A deafening crash of wood sprayed throughout the room as the Stacker was crushed to death and buried beneath tons of plain, ordinary crates. On the floor next to the steel door, half-covered with dust and shards of wood, was a sheet of paper. It read: Crates sent in error. Do not stack.

Manmade

• ELIZABETH THORPE •

Five months after she moved in, she found out why the house had been so cheap.

It started with a couple of white pickups with amber lights on top, rambling past on the dirt road. The next week, it was flatbeds with Caterpillars, and then, months later, the white blades covered in shrinkwrap like wintering boats. She watched the procession from her front porch, coffee in hand, as spring turned to summer turned to fall. She didn't like the feeling that she'd been tricked, but didn't mind the construction so much. Sure, it was sad to see the big pines fall, bounce once or twice, lie still with the dust swirling into the air around them. But at least the saws were too far away to be loud. And everyone said that windmills ruined the view, but it meant nothing else would be built on that ridge. They were better than skyscrapers, or Wal-Marts. So she watched, and rocked in her new painted rocking chair, and drank her coffee, and loved being in this house that was all her own.

For a long time she was alone, but then she met Pete at the coffee shop, and then she started seeing him there every week, and then she started going every morning, when he was most likely to be there. And then one day he said, hey, want to go see the windmills up close?

They drove up in Pete's truck, a red F-150 with the kind of paint that loses its shine after a decade or so. Pete's hands were tanned, rested casually on the steering wheel. They listened to K100, and he talked back to the DJs. The power company had done a good job with the wide, flat, road, which was smoother than the town's potholed asphalt.

She saw the first one when they rounded the corner, bigger than she had expected, like a lighthouse. Then when she stepped out of the truck, and the wind hit her full-on, she felt a rush of fear. When she got closer, when she looked straight up at the windmill and it seemed like it was falling toward her, when she saw the shadow of it against the trees behind, when the alien whirr filled her ears like it might never stop, when Pete came to stand beside her, she started to think that maybe none of this had been such a good idea.

About the SHALE Authors

Joel Allegretti was inspired to write "The Intruders" after reading a chapter of *The Coral Sea* by Patti Smith, but it has nothing whatsoever to do with Smith's text. He is still baffled as to how the one came as a result of his reading the other. Allegretti is the author of five collections of poetry. His second, *Father Silicon* (The Poet's Press, 2006), was selected by *The Kansas City Star* as one of 100 Noteworthy Books of 2006. He is the editor of *Rabbit Ears: TV Poems* (NYQ Books, 2015), the first anthology of poetry about the mass medium. Allegretti's poetry has appeared in *Barrow Street*, *Smartish Pace*, *PANK*, and many other journals. He has published fiction in *The MacGuffin*, *The Adroit Journal,* and *The Nassau Review*, among other literary journals. His performance texts and theater pieces have been staged at La MaMa Experimental Theater, Medicine Show Theater, the Cornelia Street Café, and SideWalk Café, all in New York. He is a member of the Academy of American Poets and ASCAP. His website is www.joelallegretti.com.

Peter Baroth, writer, artist, and musician, is a graduate of Washington University in St. Louis and Temple Law School. His novel is *Long Green* (iUniverse) and his poetry chapbook, *Ski Oklahoma* (Wordrunner). He won the 2009 Amy Tritsch Needle Award in poetry and is on *Philadelphia Stories'* editorial board.

Marilu Beas was born in Guadalajara and now makes her home in California. She is interested in intersections of dreams and waking narratives. She enjoys decorating and creating tableaux vivres for Halloween and other holidays.

Annie Bien received her first writing commission from the Soho Theatre Company in London, England. She has published poetry and short fiction in anthologies and magazines, and his been shortlisted in competitions. Her book of poems *Plateau Migration* was published in 2012. She is also translator of Buddhist texts from Tibetan into English with 84000, established by the Khyentse Foundation.

Peter D. Byrne is an international tax attorney who splits his time between the U.S. and Peru. He studied at Columbia University, University of the Andes (Bogota, Colombia), and Harvard Law School. He has dozens of tax-related publications, but this is his first published fiction.

Lisa J. Cihlar's poems have appeared in *Blackbird, Gargoyle Magazine, South Dakota Review, Crab Creek Review,* and *Mid-American Review*. She has been nominated for two Pushcart Prizes and a Best of the Net award. Her four chapbooks are *The Insomniac's House* from Dancing Girl Press, *This is How She Fails* and *Desire Doesn't Work Here* from Crisis Chronicles Press, and *When I Pick Up My Wings from the Dry Cleaner* from Blue Light Press. She lives in rural southern Wisconsin.

James Claffey hails from County Westmeath, Ireland, and lives on an avocado ranch in Carpinteria, CA. His first book, *blood a cold blue* will be published this fall by Press 53. His work has been featured in *Flash Fiction International Anthology* (W.W. Norton), *Best Small Fictions 2015* (Queensferry Press Anthology), and *Best of the Net 2014*.

Lydia Cortes has published two books, *Lust for Lust* (Ten Pell) and *Whose Place* (Straw Gate Books). Cortes is an "in betweener," her writing influenced by the interstices of the languages and cultures best known to her: English (New Yorkese), Spanish (Puerto Rican), Italian (Roman)—especially their poetry and fiction, their sense of reality and invention.

Daniela Elza has contributed to over 100 publications internationally. Her poetry collections are: *the weight of dew, the book of It,* and *milk tooth bane bone* of which David Abram says: "Out of the ache of the present moment, Daniela Elza has crafted something spare and irresistible, an open armature for wonder." Daniela lives and writes in Vancouver, BC.

Shinelle L. Espaillat writes, lives and teaches in Westchester County, NY. She earned her M.A. in Creative Writing at Temple University. Her work has appeared in *Midway Journal.*

Evald Flisar is a novelist, playwright, essayist, editor, globe-trotter (travelled in more than 90 countries), underground train driver in Sydney, editor of (among other publications) an encyclopaedia of science and invention in London, author of short stories and radio plays for the BBC, president of the Slovene Writers' Association (1995 - 2002). Since 1998 he has been editor of the oldest Slovenian literary journal *Sodobnost* (Contemporary Review). Author of eleven novels (six—including *If I Only Had Time*—short-listed for kresnik, the Slovenian "Booker"), two collections of short stories, three travelogues, two books for children, and fifteen stage plays. Winner of the Preseren Foundation Prize, the highest state award for prose and drama, the prestigious Zupancic Award for lifetime achievement, three awards for Best Play of the Year, etc. His works published by Texture Press include *Tales of Wandering, My Father's Dreams, The Sorcerer's Apprentice, Collected Plays, Vol. 1* and *Collected Plays, Vol. 2.*

Christine Hamm has a PhD in American Poetics, and is a former poetry editor for *Ping*Pong*. She won the MiPoesias First Annual Chapbook Competition with her manuscript, *Children Having Trouble with Meat*. Her poetry has been published in *Orbis, Pebble Lake Review, Lodestar Quarterly, Poetry Midwest, Rattle, Dark Sky*, and many others. She has been nominated five times for a Pushcart Prize, and she teaches English at Pace. *Echo Park*, her third book of poems, came out from Blazevox in the fall of 2011. As Christine was the third runner-up to the Erbacce International Poetry Prize, Erbacce published her chapbook, *My Western*, in 2012. *The New Orleans Review* published Christine's latest chapbook, *A is for Absence*, in the fall of 2014, and nominated her work for a Pushcart.

Rose Hunter is the author of three books of poetry: *You As Poetry* (Texture Press), *[four paths]* (Texture Press), and *to the river* (Artistically Declined Press). A chapbook of her poems is forthcoming from Dancing Girl Press (2015), and she will appear in the anthology *Bend River Mountain: Six Australian Poets* from Regime Books (Perth, 2015). She has been published in such journals as

Cordite, Australian Poetry Journal, Regime, Geist, New World Writing, DIAGRAM, PANK, The Nervous Breakdown, and *Press 1.* She is from Australia originally, lived in Toronto for ten years, and then in Puerto Vallarta, Mexico. More information about her is available at Whoever Brought Me Here Will Have To Take Me Home (rosehunterblog.wordpress.com).

Shalom Ikhenais a writer from Southern Nigeria. She is currently studying Economics at Drexel University and is passionate about hearing different people's stories and understanding their experiences. She also spends her free time writing on her blog: "Lattice of Love Stories (and other life happenings)"

Franklin Lafayette King, Jr. was born in the Panhandle of Texas and spent much of his youth on the Blackland Prairie. He received a commission through the University of Texas in Austin and soon became involved in the Vietnam Conflict. After additional academic preparation, he moved to the foothills of the Appalachians. In addition to combat, he experienced both the eyes of a hurricane and a F-4 tornado, events that were to influence much of his later work. He is the author of *Hauntings of a Summer Moon, Sunflowers and Zinnias, The Poet Who Writes Upon Water, In the Shadow of Leaves, The Woman in the Window, The Seven Woods of Coole, Lost Graves,* and *The Story of James and Other Writings*—all published by Texture Press.

Lynn Levin is a poet, writer, and literary translator. Her fiction has appeared in *Cleaver, Schuylkill Valley Journal, The Rag, Press 1,* and *YARN* (Young Adult Review Network). Her most recent books are a collection of poems, *Miss Plastique* (Ragged Sky Press, 2013), a Next Generation Indie Book Awards finalist in poetry; with Valerie Fox, a craft-of-poetry book *Poems for the Writing: Prompts for Poets* (Texture Press, 2013), a Next Generation Indie Book Awards finalist in education/academic books; and a translation from the Spanish, *Birds on the Kiswar Tree* (2Leaf Press, 2014), a bilingual collection of poems by Peruvian poet Odi Gonzales. Lynn Levin teaches at Drexel University and the University of Pennsylvania.

Paul Lisicky is the author of *Lawnboy, Famous Builder, The Burning House,* and *Unbuilt Projects.* His work has appeared in *Conjunctions, Denver Quarterly,*

Fence, Gulf Coast, Iowa Review, Tin House and elsewhere. His awards include fellowships from the NEA, the James Michener/Copernicus Society, and the Fine Arts Work Center in Provincetown. He's twice been a finalist for the Lambda Literary Award in both Gay Men's Fiction and in Autobiography. He teaches in the MFA Program at Rutgers University-Camden and serves as editor of *StoryQuarterly* and on the Writing Committee of the Fine Arts Work Center in Provincetown. A memoir, *The Narrow Door*, is forthcoming from Graywolf Press in January 2016.

Bobbi Lurie is the author of four poetry collections, most recently *the morphine poems*. She is currently at work on a short story collection about Marcel Duchamp.

Tara L. Masih is editor of *The RoseMetal Press Field Guide to Writing Flash Fiction* and *The Chalk Circle* (both ForeWord Books of the Year), author of *Where the Dog Star Never Glows*, and Series Editor of the annual *Best Small Fictions* anthology. Her flash has been anthologized in *Word of Mouth, Brevity & Echo, BITE, Flash Fiction Funny*, and *Stripped*, was featured in *Fiction Writer's Review* for National Short Story Month 2011, and was a finalist for the Reynolds Price Prize in Fiction. "The Mystery Spot" received a Wigleaf Top 50 award.

Mike McGilloway is a writer and musician from New Jersey. He has studied mathematics at Drexel University and performed in the band Ted Nguyent. He spends his free time reading and walking around.

Jen Michalski is the author of the novels *The Tide King* (Black Lawrence Press) and *The Summer She Was Under Water* (Queens Ferry Press), two collections of fiction, and a couplet of novellas (*Could You Be With Her Now*, Dzanc Books). Follow her on Twitter at @MichalskJen.

Susan Smith Nash started her professional life as a petroleum geologist, and then diversified by studying economics, literature, and instructional design. From Susan's perspectives, all geology, economics, and literary criticism are, on some level, "discourses of explanation," which has been helpful to her. Her explorations have given her the opportunity to satisfy her curiosity and to develop a mindset that involves the convergence of disparate elements, often in conflict. Susan earned her Bachelors of Science, Master of Arts, and Ph.D. degrees from the University of Oklahoma. Her creative publications and reviews include *Talisman, Sodobnost, World Literature Today, Gargoyle*, and others.

Liz Tynes Netto is a writer and documentary filmmaker living in Los Angeles. Her poetry and short stories have appeared in *The Mas Tequila Review, The East Jasmine Review, FRE&D*, and others.

Debi Orton is a writer and artist living on the banks of the Hudson River in rural upstate New York.

Lisa Prince is a Southern Ontarian writer who lives with her daughter, and three cats. She has had works published in several online journals, including a chapbook featured in *Lily: A Monthly Online Literary Review*, which netted her a Pushcart nomination in 2006 for Poem W. She's returned to writing after a sabbatical and is enjoying expanding her repertoire of writing skills.

Charles Rammelkamp's collection of poems, *Mata Hari: Eye of the Day*, has just been published by Apprentice House at Loyola University. A chapbook of poems, *Mixed Signals*, was published last year by Finishing Line Press. Charles edits *The Potomac*, an online literary journal—thepotomacjournal. com—and is the prose editor for BrickHouse Books in Baltimore.

Don Riggs has been writing verse of some sort for over half a century now, and the evolution of it has more to do with what was floating around in school or society at the time, although his objective is to access the Akashic Records directly and transcribe bits of them without the filter of the logosphere. He will be going to Cambridge, England, to bring John Langdon's updated version of *Alice in Wonderland* to a celebration of *Alice*'s 150th anniversary. His essay "Empire and After" appears in a collection of essays on 21st-century fantasy *Tales after Tolkien*, recently published by the Cambria Press.

John Wolfgang Roberts is a native of Los Angeles and currently lives and works in Japan. He holds an M.F.A. in fiction and has had prose and poems appear in *The GNU*, *Post Poetry*, *Bellow Literary Journal*, and *Fukushima Poetry Anthology*. He enjoys surfing, disruptive art, people-watching, and playing with his son.

Thaddeus Rutkowski is the author of the novels *Haywire*, *Tetched* and *Roughhouse*. All three books were finalists for an Asian American Literary Award, and *Haywire* won the Members' Choice award, given by the Asian American Writers Workshop. He teaches at Medgar Evers College and the Writer's Voice of the West Side YMCA in New York. He received a fiction fellowship from the New York Foundation for the Arts.

Scott Stein's novels are *Mean Martin Manning* (ENC Press 2007) and *Lost* (Free Reign Press (self-published) 2000). His satirical fiction has appeared in *National Review*, *Liberty*, and *Art Times*. He has written book reviews and essays for the *Philadelphia Inquirer* and *Liberty*. He founded and edits the online group blog/magazine whenfallsthecoliseum.com. His story "Garghibition" is anthologized in *Humor: A Reader for Writers* (Oxford University Press). He teaches at Drexel University in Philadelphia and has an MFA from the University of Miami and an MA from New York University.

Elizabeth Thorpe's short stories and excerpts from her novel-in-progress have appeared in *Per Contra*, *Painted Bride Quarterly*, *Press 1*, *Puckerbrush Review*, *Stolen Island Review*, and *The Maine Review*, among others. She is a regular contributor to the Swollen Fox and Tri State Indie music websites. She teaches Freshman Writing at Drexel University and Creative Writing in the University of the Arts Pre-College program. She earned her MFA in Writing from Goddard College.

Acknowledgements and Permissions

ALLEGRETTI, JOEL: "The Intruders" first appeared in *Thrice Fiction* in 2013. Copyright © 2013 by Joel Allegretti. Reprinted by permission of Joel Allegretti.

BAROTH, PETER: "Oil Money" appears by permission of the author. Copyright © 2015 by Peter Baroth.

BEAS, MARILU: "House of the Balustrades" appears by permission of the author. Copyright © 2015 by Marilu Beas.

BIEN, ANNIE: A variation of "Intervals in Moonglow" was published in *Touch: The Journal of Healing* (Autumn/Winter 2014). Copyright © 2014 by Annie Bien. Reprinted by permission of the author.

BYRNE, PETER D: "New Year's Eve" appears by permission of the author. Copyright © 2015 by Peter D. Byrne.

CIHLAR, LISA J.: "O' Baptism, Sings the River" appears by permission of the author. Copyright © 2015 by Lisa Cihlar.

CLAFFEY, JAMES: 8. "A Dish Best Served Unnoticed" appears courtesy of the author. Copyright © 2015 by James Claffey. "Mad Dogs & Irishmen" was published in *Press 1*. © 2012 by James Claffey. Republished by permission of the author. "Mothering" is being published by *Righthandpointing*, © 2015 by James Claffey. Republished by permission of the author.

CORTES, LYDIA: "A Lady" appears by permission of the author. Copyright

LURIE, BOBBI: "Coming Back to Earth As A Dog" was published by *Wilderness House Literary Review* in 2011. Reprinted by permission of Bobbi Lurie. "Stalking Marcel Duchamp" appears by permission of the author. Copyright © 2015 by Bobbi Lurie.

MASIH, TARA L. "The Mystery Spot" was published by *The Foundling Review* (Issue 2, July 2014). Copyright © 2014 by Tara L. Masih. Reprinted by permission of the author. "Fire-on-the-Water" was published in *Cheek Teeth*, Jan 8, 2012. Copyright © 2012 by Tara L. Masih. Reprinted by permission of the author.

MCGILLOWAY, MICHAEL: "Amps" appears by permission of the author. Copyright © 2015 by Michael McGilloway.

MICHALSKI, JEN: "Pan America" was published in *Baltimore Style Magazine*. Copyright © 2014 by Jen Michalski. Reprinted by permission of the author.

NASH, SUSAN SMITH: "Shale," "An Empty Lot Across the Street," and "Playa de los Muertos" appear by permission of the author. Copyright © 2015 Susan Smith Nash.

NETTO, LIZ TYNES: "Gray Matter" appears by permission of the author. Copyright © 2014 by Liz Tynes Netto.

ORTON, DEBI: "The Buccaneer" was previously published in 2010 in the now-defunct online journal *Kelvin*. Copyright © 2010 Debi Orton. Reprinted by permission of the author. "Fall" appears by permission of the author. Copyright © 2007 by Debi Orton.

PRINCE, LISA: "Some things I've been meaning to tell you" appears by permission of the author. Copyright © 2014 by Lisa Prince.

RAMMELKAMP, CHARLES: "Revolutions Per Minute" and "A Wise Man said Nothing" appear by permission of the author. Copyright © 2015 by Charles Rammelkamp.

• • •

With special thanks to
Melissa Rodier for her indispensable editorial assistance.

About the SHALE Editors

Arlene Ang's short stories, some co-written with Valerie Fox, have been published in *Admit Two, Juked, Monkeybicycle, Per Contra, Staccato Fiction*, and *Wigleaf*. Her latest poetry collection, *Banned for Life*, was published by Misty Publications in 2014. She lives in Spinea, Italy.

Valerie Fox was a founding editor for the magazines *6ix* and *Press 1*. Much interested in collaboration, she is recently part of group of Philadelphia artists combining dance, word, and visual arts in projects known as "Variable Space." She has published a few books with Texture Press, including *Bundles of Letters Including A, V and Epsilon*, a compilation co-written with SHALE co-editor Arlene Ang.

Nathan Leslie's eight books of fiction include *Sibs, The Tall Tale of Tommy Twice*, and *Madre*. His next book of flash fiction, *Root and Shoot*, will be published later this year by Texture Press. He is also the author of *Night Sweat*, a poetry collection. Nathan's short stories, essays and poems have appeared in hundreds of literary magazines including *Boulevard, Shenandoah, North American Review*, and *Cimarron Review*. Nathan was series editor for *The Best of the Web* anthology 2008 and 2009 (Dzanc Books) and edited fiction for *Pedestal Magazine* for five years as well. He teaches English at Northern Virginia Community College. His website is www.nathanleslie.com.

Susan Smith Nash founded Texture Press because of a love for innovative writing and self-expression, and a desire to encourage writers to cross generic and disciplinary boundaries. In addition to supporting innovative writing, she is also committed to boundary-pushing translations, influenced by Walter Benjamin, Lawrence Venuti, and Anthony Pym.